# THE DEEP END

By
GREGORY LUCE

I0616872

ARMCHAIR FICTION
PO Box 4369, Medford, Oregon   97501-0168

*For more information about Armchair Books and products, visit our
website at...*

**www.armchairfiction.com**

*Or email us at...*

**armchairfiction@yahoo.com**

# MONSTERS FROM THE WATERY DEPTHS...

*It was a summer day, 1965. On the surface everything seemed normal. A nice family pool on a hot day with dozens of children and adults splashing about. There were college and high school students on the prowl, too, looking for attractive members of the opposite sex— and none was more attractive than the new female lifeguard in the two-piece swimming suit. She sat beautifully atop her observation chair watching the events in the watery playground. But there was something strange about Graybill's swimming pool, and even more so with Jacob's Pond, which lay beyond it. A number of kids had drowned in the pond years before and now strange things were happening in the pool. It all started coming to a head when a young boy was pulled from the pool in hysterics. Something had grabbed him by the leg…*

FOR A COMPLETE SECOND NOVEL, TURN TO PAGE 71

# CAST OF CHARACTERS

### KIRBY FORRESTER
*He was just out for a swim one summer afternoon when he ran into a gorgeous, dark-haired beauty who captured his heart.*

### CARRIE MARSHFIELD
*As good-looking female lifeguards went she was a real stunner. But there was a dark mystery behind those almond-shaped eyes.*

### HENRY STOCKSTEAD
*This weather-beaten farmer was a pretty simple man, but able to keep his cool even in the most fantastic of circumstances.*

### CONNIE PARKER
*Kirby's pal and fellow employee. He was never one to put too much stock in local spook stories…until now.*

### RILEY
*This cigar-chomping police sergeant wasn't one to believe in monsters—until he ran into one face to face.*

### HAWKINS
*An old-timer who'd been around a long, long time. He knew more about local mysteries and lore than just about anybody.*

### VINCE LOCATTI
*A midnight swim with a beautiful girl sounded like a great idea…but it got him a lot more than he bargained for.*

# FOREWORD

Back in the early 1970s I was strolling around the campus book store at Southern Oregon State College (now Southern Oregon University) when I noticed a Panther Books paperback collection of H. P. Lovecraft stories staring back at me from one of the store's upper shelves. I purchased it and took it back to my room and started reading. I don't think I put it down until after midnight.

By the age of nineteen or twenty I was already a seasoned fan of horror and science fiction films. By that time I had also accumulated a huge but somewhat tattered collection of old Ace sci-fi double novels. Up to that point, though, horror literature had largely escaped me. Oh sure, I'd been forced to read Shirley Jackson's *The Lottery* by my high school English teacher; and I'd tried to read a few of the classic Poe stories but ultimately gave up on them in favor of Roger Corman's AIP films. So when I sat down and started reading *The Thing on the Doorstep* I was only vaguely aware of whom Lovecraft even was.

Over the next few days and nights I read every story in the Panther collection and overnight became a huge fan of the Cthulhu Mythos. I can remember literally getting creeped out at reading stories like *The Whisperer in Darkness, The Colour Out of Space,* and *The Haunter of the*

*Dark* late at night. Naturally, over the next few weeks I scoured every bookstore in Ashland looking for more Lovecraft. Within a few weeks I'd read just about all of his major horror tales.

I originally wrote *The Deep End* back in 1999. It's obviously inspired by Lovecraft's *The Shadow over Innsmouth*. I sent *The Deep End* out to veteran editor Bob Price, who had already published a few of my other Lovecraftian tales. Bob liked the story and it was originally published in the Chaosium Press paperback anthology, *Tales out of Innsmouth*. What a thrill it was walking into Barnes and Noble and seeing a paperback book containing one of my own stories, just scant feet away from an adjoining Starbucks!

I recently decided to reprint *The Deep End* in one of our Armchair Books. I wanted to include it as part of a double novel but it really wasn't a long-enough fit, so I sat down and hammered out this new extended version. I know, I know…the author of a story should never be the first one to sing his own praises, but I think you'll find that *The Deep End* is a pretty good read. If you like Lovecraftian tales, girls in bikinis, underwater monsters, etc. you'll probably get a kick out of it.

—*Greg Luce*
*Editor-in-chief,*
*Armchair Fiction*

# CHAPTER ONE

They pulled the boy from the pool screaming.

He was kicking and thrashing about wildly in the deep end. Everything had been peaceful just moments before, then suddenly the eight-year-old's head broke through the surface of the water and turned a typical summer day at Graybill's pool into a nightmare—screams like you couldn't imagine. Horrified looks of surprise came over everyone's faces. A couple of high school kids paddled over and tried to help the shrieking youngster to the side of the pool, but it wasn't until the new female lifeguard dove in from her rickety 10-foot platform chair that they were able to get the boy to safety.

I was lying on the ancient wooden deck that surrounded the pool, almost asleep, when the commotion broke out. *What in the sam hill?* I jerked up to find out what was happening. The sound of splashing and screams reverberated over the surface of the pool, almost drowning out the Dave Clark Five song playing in the background over the pool's loudspeaker system.

I looked over at Parker—he *was* asleep.

"Connie...wake up!" I reached over and shook him. He woke up with a start.

"Damn...who's dyin'?" he asked as he sat up. We both looked over just in time to see them drag the boy— kicking and screaming—out of the pool.

"What the heck is his problem?" I said.

Connie just shook his head and got a weird look on his face. We both got up and started moving toward the frenzied youngster. There was already a crowd gathering around him, including a couple of other lifeguards and a number of older adults. The boy had stopped screaming by now but was still babbling hysterically. He kept repeating the same thing over and over...

*"It grabbed my leg! It grabbed my leg!"*

I looked over at Connie: the look on his face got even weirder. As we tried to move in closer, a crouched figure suddenly straightened up and turned toward us. "Please stand back," she said.

It was the new female lifeguard.

At that moment I got my first real good look at her; I felt a mild rush of physical attraction. *Hmm. Not bad.* She was probably about my age—20 or 21. A two-piece not-quite-a-bikini swimsuit helped show off her trim, very attractive physique; and a mane of long, sleek, wet black hair touched the top of her shoulder blades. Her face was somewhat thin—a perfect contrast to those beautiful almond-shaped brown eyes. I couldn't tell if she was naturally dark or just had a good tan that summer, but it looked as though she might have some kind of foreign blood in her, like a Hawaiian native or some other South Sea Islander.

"What's wrong with the kid," Connie asked her.

"He's just hysterical," she replied. "Some punk probably grabbed his foot and held him under too long. He probably panicked." She looked back at the huddle: The boy seemed to be calming down a little. "I think he's going to be okay. Why don't you just stand back and let us take care of him."

She motioned the rest of the throng of onlookers to back up as well. A minute or two later, the boy was carried out by a husky-looking lifeguard, accompanied by a couple of other pool employees. As quickly as it had started, it was suddenly over. Swimmers began hopping back in the pool and resuming their sunbathing positions on the pool deck. Connie and I laid back down on our towels to catch a few more rays.

"That was weird, man," he said.

"No big deal. Just a screamin' kid."

"Gimme a break, Kirby. That kid went bonkers. It even gave *me* the creeps. Somethin' scared him bad…real bad."

I didn't say anything. I just raised my head and glanced over toward the deep end. The Hire's Root Beer thermometer on the fence by the high-dive read 97 degrees. The new female lifeguard had climbed back atop her rickety observation chair and was just sitting there, motionless, peering over that end of the pool. The sun was hanging behind her and made her look like a big black silhouette with sunglasses.

I leaned over and nudged Connie in the ribs. "Listen…maybe you're right," I said, half-smiling. "Maybe there's something down there that scared the crap out of that kid…something on the bottom…" I raised my eyebrows and widened my eyes, "…something…*inhuman*."

Connie glanced up and got that weird look on his face again.

"Come on," I continued, "let's dive in and see what's down there."

"Forget it, man. I'm practically dry."

I got up anyway and hopped into the shallow end. The aroma of chlorine was strong. I dodged my way around a group of rowdy Wa-High kids having a major splash fight and slowly waded down toward the deeper end of the pool. Graybill's was basically an old, dilapidated facility built around the turn of the century, but it was well known by local swimmers for having the deepest deep end in town, bottoming out at nearly 13 feet. There was a buoyed plastic rope that separated the main body of the pool from the deep end; it ran across the width of the pool, bobbing up and down in the choppy water. I paused on the shallow side, then took a deep breath and dove under the rope. As I kicked down toward the bottom, I could feel the pressure rising in my ears like a couple of big hands were trying to squeeze my brains out. I started feeling around on the bottom with my fingers—the cement was cold and slimy.

Then I noticed it.

In one corner there appeared to be a dark, circular area, a couple of feet wide with something protruding out of it. After heading to the surface and grabbing another breath, I shot back down for a closer look. I was surprised to discover what appeared to be some type of round, rubber-sealed door, or portal, a few feet away from the main drain. It was made out of metal— probably iron—and had a handle on one side of it. I gave it a good rap with my knuckles. It sounded solid. Then I grabbed the handle to give it a tug. It seemed a little loose. Right as I began to pull, a hand suddenly reached in and grabbed my wrist. *What the hell!* I practically had a heart attack; my head jerked around…

It was the female lifeguard.

I lost my breath and kicked back suddenly. She was just hovering there near the bottom, staring at me with those almond eyes, shaking her head and pointing a finger. My lungs were ready to burst so I shot back to the top, gasping for air as I broke through the surface. I swam over and hung onto the side of the pool, trying to catch my breath. She broke through the water next to me and looked at me apologetically.

"Sorry if I scared you."

"For cryin' out loud, man. I almost peed in your pool."

She tried to suppress a smile. "That's exactly what I thought you were going to do there for a second or two."

"Why did you grab my arm?"

Her eyes glanced downward. "Nobody's supposed to fool around with the old drainage gate on the bottom."

"Drainage gate?"

"Yeah. The one that leads over to Jacob's Pond on the other side of the hill. That's how they used to empty the pool…years ago."

"I'll remember that next time."

"Thanks. Please do."

She flashed an attractive smile that helped me get over my momentary fright. I once again felt that mild rush of physical attraction that I had felt earlier.

"You're new here, aren't you?" I asked.

"I've been a lifeguard here since the beginning of July, but I've been swimming here for years. You a regular?"

"Only this season. I'm a senior over at Whitman, and I'm usually in Tacoma during the summer months. This year I decided to stick around for summer school."

"Steep tuition," she commented.

"You can say that again. I work part-time as a board-op over at TV-26, too."

"What's a board-op?"

"Uh…somebody who sits behind a control console and makes sure that everything goes on the air that's supposed to. You know…network feeds, local commercials…that kind of thing."

"Sounds interesting." She looked me over with those almond eyes for the next few seconds, then said, "Well…gotta get back to my chair." She smiled again and climbed out of the pool.

I just hung there on the side…watching, ogling. She was a beautiful young woman. If you're a 21-year old male with a high testosterone level, there's nothing quite like having a shapely female figure slide up out of the water next to you. I could see her wet, beautiful tan skin glistening in the sunlight, the moisture beading up on the back of her long, lovely legs. When you're that close and you stare hard enough, it's almost as though you can see *through* the swimsuit.

I stared hard—*real* hard.

She sensed it, too. She stood above me for several seconds, wringing out her hair. As she starting climbing back up into her rickety chair, I called out to her:

"Hey…what's your name?"

She stopped in mid-climb and stared down at me before answering.

"Carrie…Carrie Marshfield," she replied, that attractive smile slowly creasing her mouth again.

I watched her slide back into the chair before I climbed out of the pool. As I walked back over toward Connie, I thought I saw her steal a glance in my direction. When I got back to my towel, Connie was sound asleep. I poked him softly in the ribs with my big toe.

"Connie, wake up."

His head tilted up slightly. "What is it, man?"

"What do you know about the new female lifeguard?" I asked.

"I don't know anything," he replied, glancing in her direction. "She ain't no dog, though…that's for sure. You interested?"

"Oh…I'm not sure. Maybe."

"Ask Hawkins about her, he'll know." Connie nodded toward the snack-stand at the opposite side of the pool where an old, white-haired concessionaire was busy pulling sodas and selling candy.

"I'll catch him when we leave," I said as I laid back down.

A little later Connie and I stopped at the concession stand on the way out of the pool. Hawkins was a real Walla Walla old-timer and loved to talk. He didn't know much about Carrie Marshfield except that she seemed to be a little on the quiet side and always walked to work. He too, was impressed with her physical attributes.

"Nice ass and nice legs," he said, raising his bushy eyebrows up and down.

"She was telling me something about an old drainage flume on the bottom of the pool that leads over to some pond," I said.

"Jacob's Pond." Hawkins nodded and pointed over his shoulder. "Just over that rocky rise and down the slope behind the back side of the pool…'bout a hundred yards or so."

Connie's eyebrow's raised. "Jacob's Pond…man, that's where all those kids drowned back in the '50s. I used to go swimming there myself…before they closed it off. That's where *all* the kids went that didn't have pool money. I got chased outa' there plenty a' times."

The crusty old concessionaire rolled his eyes from side to side as he reached back into his aging memory banks. "Ten years ago to be exact…summer of '55. Three kids in three months…" Hawkins' voice lowered a bit, "…but who said they drowned?"

Connie looked perplexed. "What do mean?"

"I mean they never found any of the bodies."

For the third time that afternoon, Connie got a weird look on his face. "Why do you say that?"

Hawkins shifted his Yankees baseball cap back on his head and wiped his brow with a paper napkin. "Well…I'm not a geologist, so I don't know how to explain it from a scientific point of view, but as I understand it, Jacob's Pond ain't got no bottom…it ain't no regular pond. If you've been there you know what I'm talkin' about. Nothing mainly but a bunch a' rock slabs with dirt and water sittin' on top of 'em. Peculiar thing is though, once you get out into the center of the pond, it drops off…some kind of a big hole…goes straight down hundreds a' feet. That's why they never found those kids' bodies. If they did drown, they're still churnin' around down there somewhere. I remember the Army Corps of Engineers sent some divers down not long after the last kid disappeared. Couldn't find nothin' except more water. They did come up with some kinda cockeyed theory, though."

"What was that?" Connie asked.

"They said the pond was being fed water by some deep, deep underground stream. Lord only knows where they thought that came from. They fenced the pond off not long after that. There's barbed wire and 'no trespassing' signs all around the place."

"Why did they quit using the old drainage flume?" I asked.

"Used to give 'em back-up problems whenever we had wet summers," Hawkins answered. "You see, the level of the pond is normally a quite a bit lower than the level of the pool. We used to use the drainage flume to the pond occasionally—not all the time—but just occasionally. There was some cockeyed plumbing reason why we had to use it once in a while and I'll be darned if I can remember what it was. Anyway, sometimes during rainy summers…especially after a hard winter…the pond level got too high and backed up dirty water into the pool. Caused all kind a' problems."

Hawkins got a hesitant look on his face. He seemed to be having second thoughts about what he was going to say next. Finally, he continued:

"Another thing, too…"

"What's that," I asked.

"The last couple a' years before they shut off that drain, the water from the pond changed."

Connie looked at him quizzically. "Changed? What do you mean? How?"

Hawkins leaned forward and grimaced. "Stunk to high heaven. You could really smell it when it backed up into the pool, too. They shut us down a few times because of it. That was back in '57. You can still smell it comin' over the rise now and then…'specially when there's a breeze comin' in from the southeast. Almost makes you wanna puke."

Hawkins paused and lowered his voice again…

"Bad place…Jacob's Pond."

Connie and I just looked at each other. By this time we *both* had weird looks on our faces.

# CHAPTER TWO

The eleven o'clock news was just starting. I hit the audio cart that started the show's intro: *And now...the Inland Empire's most comprehensive newscast...Action News at eleven, with anchorman, Dick Hoover...*

Connie punched in camera one; his finger cued Hoover.

*"Good evening. In our headline story tonight, another young man has turned up missing in the Walla Walla area."*

I was a startled by Hoover's lead-in and looked up in surprise. Hoover must have seen my jaw drop, because he stumbled over his next word or two before continuing with his disturbing story.

*"22-year old Arthur Benefield was officially listed as a missing person by the Walla Walla Police Department today after his employers reported his disappearance Wednesday afternoon. Benefield's vehicle was found earlier today, parked on the south edge of town. Neighborhood residents say the abandoned 1963 Ford Ranchero had been sitting in the same spot since at least last Monday evening, almost two days before Benefield's employers reported him missing."*

This was the fourth guy to turn up missing in a little less than two months. Local authorities had found not a trace of any of the others, either. I looked over at Connie—that same familiar weird expression was coming over his face. I leaned toward him and whispered.

"Can you believe this? That's four since June. What's this all about anyway?"

Connie shook his head. "I don't know, but heads are gonna roll downtown if the cops can't figure this thing out soon. I mean how often does something like this happen in a town this size?"

"Practically never."

"Exactly."

We sat and listened to the rest of the story. Benefield's deserted pickup had been found out on School Avenue just outside the city limits. The police had examined it thoroughly but turned up nothing in the way of clues. There was no blood, no vandalism—no signs of violence of any kind.

"How much you wanna bet that pickup was parked there by somebody else," I whispered.

Connie looked at me quizzically. "What do you mean?"

"Just a hunch," I said.

Connie whispered back, "Well, whoever the hell it is, it's gotta be more than one person. I mean these are all young guys that are disappearing...probably not a bunch a' wimps, either. A lone kidnapper's gonna have a pretty hard a time handling all four of these guys without any trouble."

"Yeah...unless he's got a knife in their ribs or a gun to their heads. Besides, what makes you think these are all kidnappings? Maybe it's just some nut, a small town spree killer...who knows? I mean nobody's found any ransom notes so far. Heck, I don't think they've even found any actual clues yet, have they?"

"Not that I've heard of."

"So what gives?"

Connie didn't answer; he just shook his head and shrugged his shoulders.

"There's more to this than anyone knows," I said.

The rest of the newscast flowed smoothly. After the end of the show I fired up the National Anthem tape and signed the station off the air. A few minutes later I was punching my timecard and heading down the stairs to the front door of the station. It was fast approaching midnight.

My car was parked up Main Street about a block away. As I walked in that direction I noticed another a car parked alongside the curb just up from the Liberty Theater. The Liberty was a beautiful old movie palace built back in the '40s. There were double features every evening that usually got out around the time we shut the station down for the night. The car parked in front was a '56 Chevy Bel Air with its hood up. Standing in front of the vehicle in the shadow of the raised hood was a darkened figure.

I slowed my pace a little as I approached, walking as softly as I could. Whoever it was hadn't heard my footsteps. They were bending over, looking over the engine with a flashlight. I came to a complete stop as the person came into full view. I cleared my throat and spoke softly.

"Need some help?"

There was a momentary look of surprise on the person's face as she looked up at me, then a slow smile of recognition crossed her face.

"Why yes," Carrie Marshfield replied. "Thanks very much."

"It's you," I said, somewhat surprised, "the lifeguard from the pool."

"You remember. I'm flattered," she responded. "I'm not too surprised, though. After all you couldn't seem to get your eyes off me the other day."

I was a little embarrassed by her directness. "Well— you know—I mean—uh—"

She turned her head and giggled softly. "Yeah, I know. I get that kind of thing from a lot of the guys at the pool, especially when I wear my two-piece."

Your name's Carrie isn't it? Carrie Mmm—"

"Marshfield…it's Carrie Marshfield" she said, a coy smile on her face.

"Yeah, that's right…Marshfield. My name's Kirby. Kirby Forrester." I stuck my hand out. "It's nice to meet you."

She took my hand and shook it for a moment or two. I didn't want to let go. Her hand was soft and warm and I was feeling that same rush of physical attraction I'd felt the other day. There was an awkward moment of silence while I gawked at her beautiful face. She just stared back and smiled.

Finally I said, "You know you almost scared me to death when you grabbed my arm at the bottom of the pool."

"Well…now you weren't supposed to be tugging on that handle, were you?"

"Nope…guess not. And you sure let me know about it, didn't you?" We laughed a little, then I glanced under the hood of her vehicle. "Well…what's going on with your car? Anything I can do to help?"

"I don't know," she replied. "I came out of the Liberty just a little while ago and it wouldn't start. I'm afraid I'm not much of a mechanic."

"Don't feel bad," I grinned back, "neither am I. I can give you a lift, though."

"Thanks. I appreciate it. I'll leave it here tonight and have somebody come out and look at it in the morning. Can you take me home?"

"You bet."

A few moments later we were speeding across town, talking all the way. I was feeling a growing fascination for this beautiful girl who was sitting just mere inches away from me.

Carrie lived in a house just outside the city limits, a couple of hundred yards down Kendall road from Graybill's pool, which explained what Hawkins had meant about Carrie always walking to work.

I pulled up in front and killed the engine. Carrie looked over at me and said, "Thanks for the ride. See you at the pool some time…"

"Can I walk you up to your door?"

She smiled at this, as though she had expected it. "Sure," she replied. "C'mon…"

I came around and opened her door. I could tell she was amused at my chivalry. We walked up to the front porch and crossed to the main doorway.

"Thanks again," she said, turning to look at me.

"My pleasure," I responded. "Listen, Carrie…"

"Yes…?"

I looked kind of awkwardly off to one side, not sure exactly what I was going to say. I'm sure she could tell I was blushing a little, even in the dim light.

Finally I mustered my courage and said, "Would you like to have…lunch sometime…maybe?"

She got a really big smile on her face at this. "Sure, Kirby…I'd love to. Call me up sometime. Jackson-9-3325."

Then she leaned forward and kissed me on the cheek.

# CHAPTER THREE

I went crazy over Carrie Marshfield.

It started out with an innocent lunch date at the A&W the day after her car trouble—a Mama Burger, a Papa Burger, two root beer floats, and some easy chit chat in my '59 Fairlane. Two days later we had dinner and a movie. By the end of the week there was another date and things were already starting to get steamy.

"You meet all the qualifications," she'd tell me with a smile.

She started spending occasional nights at my apartment, some really memorable nights, too—the kind of stuff bachelor pipe dreams are made of. I was swept off my feet by her unpretentious disposition and sexual magnetism. In a matter of days she had me completely infatuated; by the end of the second week I was already pondering marriage. I mentioned it to Connie one night at the station.

"You gotta have rocks in your head," he told me, "Marriage?"

I shrugged my shoulders and gave him a goofy smile.

Connie shook his head, laughing under his breath. "C'mon, Kirby. I mean…granted…she's a babe…but this is crazy. Are you really gonna hang it up for this broad? Permanently?"

I shrugged my shoulders again. Connie lectured for another minute or two, but I wasn't really listening. All I could think about was that gorgeous, sleek body inside that skimpy, dripping not-quite-a-bikini swimsuit.

"You're hopeless," he finally told me, looking down at the control console.

One evening, about a week later, Carrie dropped by unexpectedly and asked me out on a double date.

"Why would I want to share you with a couple of other people?" I asked.

"Cause I've got something up my sleeve," she replied, leveling a hard, knowing smile at me. "And you're gonna like it."

"Like it? Like what?"

"It's a secret."

I rolled my eyes from side to side. "Secret?"

"Uh-huh. And you can't tell anybody we're going out. I've got something special planned and nobody else can know about it...okay?"

"Are you kidding? A *secret* date?" I folded my hands behind my head and leaned back in the chair. "I've never been on a *secret* date before. What did you have in mind...an orgy in Pioneer Park or something?"

She winked. "Be good and you'll find out Saturday night. Come by late."

"How late?"

"Make it around eleven o'clock. It'll be you and me and Helen."

Who's coming with Helen?" I asked, referring to Carrie's younger sister.

"Nobody you know. You'll find out Saturday." She leaned forward and pecked a quick kiss on my cheek. "Oh, by the way…"

"Yeah?"

"…be sure to bring your swim trunks."

Carrie turned and dashed out the door, leaving me wondering about what she had planned for the coming weekend.

That Saturday evening I cruised out toward the Marshfield house in my green '59 Fairlane. Carrie and Helen lived there with their invalid father, Homer Marshfield.

Homer had been severely crippled for a number of years, some type of grisly cannery accident involving a conveyer belt—very unpretty. He was confined to a wheelchair and never left the house that I knew of. In fact, according to Carrie he rarely came out of his bedroom. I used to see him occasionally peering out of his bedroom window on the third floor. One day as I drove up I saw his bushy face staring down at me. He rolled back into the shadows when he saw me look up and wave. Another time I heard his voice echoing down the stairwell near the end of the foyer. It had an odd sound, similar to the frog-like croaks of someone who's had their larynx removed. I was quietly glad we never met.

I made the turn onto Kendall road and passed by Graybill's pool. I could see the moonlight shimmering off the smooth surface of the water. Just up ahead was the Marshfield place. The house itself was a crumbling old three-story affair with gabled windows protruding through the roof on the third floor. A pair of large, aging Sycamore trees obscured much of the structure from view. I had only been inside of it a scant number of times and then only in the main parlor, Carrie and I having spent most of our time over at my apartment or out on dates. As I pulled into the driveway, I saw Carrie sitting on the front porch swing, waving to me in the brilliant light of the full moon that blanketed the countryside.

I killed the motor; Carrie called out to me playfully, "Get a horse!"

My hands went up on the steering wheel and gripped it tightly. "Take me as I am, baby."

"You're such a retard," she laughed back, "but you do meet all the qualifications." She waved me toward the porch.

Sitting next to Carrie was Helen and her date, a bodybuilder-type named Vince Locatti. Locatti was a blue collar stud who practically broke my hand as he rose to meet me.

"Glad to know you, Kirby," he said with a smirk, squeezing my metacarpals as hard as he could.

Helen was fairly attractive, but not near so much as her sister Carrie. She was noticeably quieter, too, and didn't smile much, her personality being hidden behind a mane of exceptionally long black hair that usually covered half of her face. She was pretty, yet somewhat odd-looking. She had a funny way of tilting her head sometimes when she spoke to you.

"Nice to see you again, Kirby," she said with that odd crook in her neck.

Carrie walked past her and embraced me. "Bring your trunks?" she asked.

I held up a pair of ragged cut-offs. "These'll have to do."

The four of us soon wandered across the open field between the Marshfield house and Graybill's pool. Carrie used her employee's key to open the main entrance and the doors to the men and women's locker rooms.

"Remember, don't turn on any lights except for the overhead in the locker room while you're changing your clothes, and be sure to keep the door closed," she told Vince and me. "Can't chance being seen by somebody driving by. The Sheriff's Department loves to prowl up and down these country roads in the middle of the night."

Vince and I quietly sneaked into the men's locker room. It was old and it had the usual locker room aroma: a mixture of chlorine and human body odors. We flipped on a dull yellow light that hung from the ancient wooden rafters and started to change. Locatti peeled off his shirt revealing a muscle-rippled olive-skinned physique. It made me feel a little inhibited about taking my clothes off.

"Where in town do you live?" I asked him.

Locatti shook his head. "Not from around here...from Kennewick. Been over here weekends on a construction job. Just finished up today."

"How long have you known Helen?"

"Not long at all," he said, pulling his trunks up over his jock strap. "I camp out over at the Marcus Whitman Hotel when I'm in town. The company pays for it all...you know. Anyway, I met her in the hotel lounge last Saturday night. We had a couple a' drinks and talked for awhile." He got a big mile-wide grin on his face. "She said she wanted to see me again this weekend. So here I am."

"Great night for a midnight swim," I replied.

We finished changing and went poolside.

# CHAPTER FOUR

It was a midnight swim under the brightest full moon you could imagine.  Graybill's pool took on an entirely different persona in the warm lunar glow.  It was a soft ambiance that reeked of ashen beauty.  The aged, rickety wooden buildings looked somehow newer, the softness of light hiding the defects and scars of age.  Even the peeling painted image of an old-time bathing beauty on the side of the main building looked fresh and new.

The water was amazingly warm for this time of night, especially considering Graybill's was a non-heated pool.  Vince and Helen were the first to dive in.  They splashed around the deep end, hopping in and out and laughing and screaming like a couple of grade school kids.  Carrie and I stayed mainly toward the shallow end, holding each other in long wet embraces.  The distorted, dancing images of the full moon reflected into my eyes off the surface of the choppy water.

"Beautiful night," I commented.

"Glad you're enjoying it," she responded warmly.

"Glad to be here."

She kissed me softly on the mouth.

Before long we climbed out of the pool and stretched out on the wooden deck, snuggling under a huge beach towel and holding each other close.  Carrie laid on top of me and nibbled at my ears and neck.  Presently she sat up, still on top of me, and shook the limp hair out of her face, the beach towel falling from her shoulders onto my lower legs. I had never seen her so beautiful. The warm moonlight gave her an unusual, pallid beauty.

I laid my hands behind my head and said, "So this was your big secret."

"Well...I wasn't sure how my boss would react if he knew one of his lifeguards was throwing a private midnight pool party."

"Just how long have you been a lifeguard, anyway?"

"For a few years." Carrie rolled off and sat up. "Since high school. Used to work over at Memorial. I like it here better, though."

I leaned up on an elbow. "So where did you learn to swim so well?"

Carrie stared at me blankly before answering. "Innsmouth."

"In what?"

"Innsmouth...it's a town. I used to live there when I was younger. We moved here about 10 years ago."

"Never been there," I said, shaking my head. "Never even heard of it."

"I'm not surprised. It's a little village on the coast of Massachusetts." She hesitated and gave me an odd expression, then said, "I'll take you there someday."

I raised my eyebrows. "Will you now?"

Carrie leaned over and gave me a half-smile. "Sooner than you think."

A curious remark, I thought. I was about to respond when something caught my attention from the other end of the pool. Helen and Vince had been laughing and splashing around in the deep end for several minutes. All at once I heard Vince cry out with surprise.

"My foot! There's someth—" His voice gurgled out, cut off as though he had been dunked under water in mid-sentence. I glanced over. Vince was nowhere in sight. All I could see was Helen treading water in the deep end. She was still laughing a little, but after a few seconds she grew quiet—just treading water, saying nothing, staring right back at me, that funny tilt in her head even in the water.

It struck me as queer, so I rolled over and called out to her, "Helen...where's Vince? Everything all right?"

She didn't say a word.

I stared out over the pool for the next few seconds, waiting for Vince to resurface. He didn't. I called out again, "What happened to Vince...where is he?"

Helen just continued to tread water in the moonlight, still staring in my direction. There was no expression on her face of any kind that I could see. I didn't know what to think. *This had better be some kind of a joke.* A wave of uneasiness rolled up my spine and suddenly I wasn't feeling romantic anymore. Something wasn't right. I started to get up, then I saw Helen kick up a little and dive under the surface. I looked down at Carrie; she was sitting there cross-legged, staring at me blankly—exactly like Helen. The strangest expression was on her face.

"Carrie...what's goin—"

Before I could finish I was cut off by the sound of splashing at the other end of the pool. I looked over—it was Vince. He was back up again, yelling at the top of his lungs.

"Carrie! Kirby! Help! Something's trying to pull me down!"

Before he could say anything else he was yanked under again. I broke toward the pool, but before I could dive in he resurfaced. This time he appeared to have broken free of whatever it was that had grabbed him and was swimming as fast as he could in my direction, toward the shallow end. I hopped down the pool stairs and started wading quickly toward him. He had covered about 30 yards and was well past the middle of the pool, only a few yards away. Suddenly his speed slowed. My arms reached out—I was practically touching him. What happened next made me freeze with sudden, intense fright.

Locatti started moving backwards.

He was still swimming toward me as hard as he could, but his movement was in the opposite direction, like a car with no chains, spinning its wheels madly as it slides down an icy hill in the dead of winter. The warm summer evening air suddenly seemed cold and I began to tremble as I realized what was happening…

*Something was dragging him down from under the surface—backwards, back toward the deep end.*

Locatti's arms flailed frantically, but to no avail. His face rose out of the water and looked up at me in a contorted, pleading look of absolute horror.

"For Pete's sake, Kirby, help me! They're comin' out of a hole in the bottom of the pool! Help me…quick! *Help m*—" His voice cut out again as he slid under the surface.

"Vince! *Vince!*" I yelled frantically. I looked back in Carrie's direction. She was standing at the top of the stairs now, motionless, like a picturesque statue radiating with a warm moonglow. The look on her face was like a statue's, too—cold, almost blank. I was suddenly very pissed at her.

"Carrie...you're a lifeguard, dammit! Get in here and help! Come on!"

I turned and splashed toward the middle of the pool, but a dim flicker of movement beneath the surface brought me to a dead stop. My eyes locked in on the body of water in front of me.

Most people go through their lives without ever knowing what it means to be really horrified, scared so bad you can take your own pulse without fingering for it, your ears being able to feel that pumping, pounding high-pressure rhythm all up and down your body. On that warm summer night under a beautiful full moon I felt that kind of cold, raw terror for the first time. As I stood there in the middle of Graybill's pool at midnight staring toward the deep end, I could see four shadowy figures, all under water, swimming rapidly in my direction. They were all converging on the very spot I was standing, moving quickly—very quickly. I turned my head and screamed.

*"Holy shit!"*

I whirled around and started splashing as rapidly as I could back toward the pool steps. It was then that I saw Carrie descending the stairs toward me. I waved my arms frantically.

"Get back! Something's after me!"

There was no concern on her face, though. She waded into the shallow end, moving smoothly and quietly toward me in the glimmering moonlight, that cold look still on her face, those almond eyes staring blankly, straight into mine.

She intercepted me a few yards from the bottom of the stairs. I almost fell headfirst into the shallow water between us as I charged toward her, but she reached out and grabbed me by the shoulders. The coldness suddenly disappeared from her face and she smiled. A big smile, a wide smile—it was probably the widest smile I had ever seen on her face. Not a smile of warmth and affection, though, it was a smile of someone who's committed a treacherous act—a smile of betrayal.

"You meet all the qualifications," she said.

Her words froze me in my tracks. This wasn't the same girl that had been kissing me passionately minutes before. She was different now...*changed*. Carrie's arms reached up and wrapped around my neck. "I have something to share with you, Kirby...some secrets to tell." The moonlight fell across her beautiful face as she moved forward to kiss me. Something was wrong, though, horribly wrong.

So I punched her in the stomach.

She gasped and bent over, her face almost slapping into the water. The ridges of her vertebrae glistened in the moonlight. She hadn't expected me to do anything like that. Neither had I for that matter. This was the woman I loved. My thoughts were chaotic.

*Are you crazy?*

Then the woman I loved looked up and gave me the most awful expression of animalistic rage you could ever imagine. No more smiles, no more affection in those almond eyes—there was no way to describe it.

So I punched her again.

This time she crumpled completely and sunk down into the water, her head dipping below the surface. I rushed past her toward the pool stairway. As I reached the top stair I looked over my shoulder and saw the four underwater figures streak past her just as she was straightening up again. She turned and pointed a stiff arm in my direction.

"Get him!"

I didn't wait around to see who was supposed to get me. I scrambled out of the pool area as fast as I could. Behind me I could hear the noise of someone—or some *thing*—splashing up out of the pool. I flew into the men's locker room at full speed, slipped, and fell on my ass. In the dim light from overhead I could see a sign on the wall staring back at me:

NO RUNNING.

I hopped up and snagged my Converse low-tops off the wooden dressing bench and bolted for the entrance. I got outside and slammed the door behind me, pausing just long enough to slip my shoes on. The sound of wet footsteps approaching from the other side of the door made my eyes grow wide. There were voices, too— gurgling, barking sounds that were unintelligible to me. I streaked across the parking lot and cut back through the open field toward the Marshfield house. I had to get to my Fairlane. I had to get the hell out of there.

As I scurried up the rise near the north side of the house, I slowed up a little and looked over my shoulder. At a distance of about 40 yards I could see four figures loping in pursuit. I couldn't really see them clearly, but they were running in an odd manner that reminded me of how an ape might run, not at a fast gait, but at a quick, steady shuffle; and although I was sure they were losing ground on me, I continued running as hard as I could. I lost sight of them as I sped over the rise and down the slope toward the house. Right at the Marshfield property line, a field mouse scampered in front of me and nearly gave me a heart attack; I practically fell head over heals trying to dodge it. I regained my balance and moved in toward the backside of the house where there was a large, overgrown hedge lining the upper end of the driveway. My nostrils suddenly flared—an incredibly foul stench was in the air. I crept up behind the hedge. Here the stench was even stronger. My Fairlane was only a few yards away, though, just on the other side. Then it hit me.

My pants—and car keys—were still hanging back in the locker room.

"Dammit!" I cursed under my breath.

I peered over the top of the bushes. In front of me was something that made me suddenly forget about my keys. The Fairlane was sitting about twenty yards down the driveway, but standing around it were three figures; this time I got a good look at them and cringed in horror. Before me were three utterly inhuman creatures that appeared to be guarding my car. They were all fish-like in appearance: sloped, apish heads, protruding mouths, webbed hands and feet, and scaly green skin, except for a bloated, white belly. They looked like they had literally stepped off the set of *The Creature From the Black Lagoon* (which Carrie and I had seen on TV just a few nights earlier—her favorite movie).

I was completely winded so my breathing was heavy and loud, and I was afraid the creatures on the other side of the hedge would hear me. Ever try to breathe quietly when you're completely out of breath? Forget it. It's nearly impossible without fainting for lack of oxygen, but I tried anyway, backing slowly away from the hedge, hoping the fish-men around my beloved Fairlane wouldn't hear me. In the distance I could hear the barking and baying sounds of the other creatures approaching from the far side of the rise.

I had to get moving again.

The fish-men near my car were standing roughly between me and Kendall road—no escape that way—so I turned and sprinted across the open field to the east. Wilbur Avenue was a few hundred yards in that direction. I'd find a house and call the cops. I ran quietly toward a clump of chestnut trees that lay well behind the Marshfield house. My lungs were screaming for oxygen by this time. It felt like high school track all over again. When I came into the trees I slowed my pace. It was nearly pitch black. Very little light crept through the twisted branches above and I was afraid of tripping and falling on my ass again. Cold, unfriendly moonlight washed over me once more as I stepped out of the trees.

Lying in front of me was Jacob's Pond.

I could see it fairly clearly. On the other side of the barbed wire fence around the edge of the pond must have been a dozen or more of the scaly fish-men. Some of them were diving into the pond; some of them were climbing out—monster's night at the old swimming hole. My nose twitched again as more of the foul smell drifted into my nostrils, the same smell as the driveway. Then a slimy hand grabbed my shoulder and spun me around.

I was nose to nose with a fish-man.

I screamed and stumbled backwards as it went for my throat. My legs faltered, but I dodged haphazardly to the side and ended up on the ground as the creature lunged past me. It made an unholy baying noise as it whirled around. The earth beneath my hands was dry and loose so I scooped up a handful and threw at its face as it came for me again. It bayed a guttural scream and doubled up in obvious pain as the dirt sliced into its eyes. While it was leaning over, I saw my chance. I jumped to my feet and kicked it on the side of the head as hard as I could. It grunted and tottered for a moment, just long enough for me to kick it again. It tumbled to the ground and I sprinted off as fast as I could. I didn't know if it was still after me or not, I just kept running. My lungs were wheezing; the adrenaline was pumping; and I kept running and running, the dry summer soil crunching beneath my feet.

I finally took a moment to look back as I went over a slight crest in the field. There didn't appear to be anyone following me, so I turned and ran on. There was an old wooden fence up ahead. I cleared it in one flying leap and landed in the soft dirt beyond. It was a plowed field. I trudged forward, but I was spent, all in. Sweat dripped off me and my head throbbed with distress.

*Carrie...Carrie...what the hell were you up to? What were you trying to do to me?*

I almost felt like crying. My feet sunk into the soft, plowed earth as I plodded ahead. It was like running in a nightmare—pumping hard, getting nowhere. I was moving south now, parallel to Kendall road, away from Graybill's—away from town. Up on my right I noticed the driveway light of a farmhouse. It was on the far side of Kendall Road. I had a sudden feeling of hope.

A telephone.

I angled off in that direction, crossed the road, and scurried up the porch. I slammed my fist repeatedly on the door...

# CHAPTER FIVE

Even though it was after midnight, there was a dim light inside. I thought I could hear the muffled sound of a television so I kept pounding on the door, looking around every few seconds to see if I had been pursued. Presently I heard the sound of approaching footsteps. A porch-light went on overhead. Then a muffled male voice sounded through the door.

"What d'ya want?"

"I need help. I'm from town. I—I need to call the police."

There was no response.

"Please…you can make the call for me. I'll stand out here on the porch."

A few more seconds went by, then I got my answer.

"Ain't got no telephone."

"Uh…well…can you let me in? I'm in trouble…I really need help."

"What kind of trouble?"

"I'm being chased."

"Who's chasin' ya?"

What a predicament. There was no way he'd open the door if I told him the truth. I could just hear it. "Hey buddy, I've got four scaly monsters trying to kick my ass and take me for a late night swim in Jacob's Pond." Right. Even if he did open the door I'd probably have a shotgun zeroed in on the middle of my nose, ready to turn my skull into a cranial sinkhole. Then again he might have a baseball bat, which would be even better: "Louisiana Slugger" emblazoned across my forehead—no thanks.

So I lied.

"There's some guys chasing me. They—they jumped me…and my girlfriend…down by the pool. I think they're still after me…but I—I'm not really sure…I just need your help…*please*."

A key turned in the latch; the door swung open; and a man stepped out onto the porch. He was big—well over six feet and at least 200 pounds. Fortyish. There was a lot of hard work in his face like so many other farmers in the area. He had a Pacific Trails wind breaker on and his right hand was in one of the pockets—a pistol, I figured. He looked me over with eyes permanently squinted by too much field dust.

He pulled his hand out of his pocket: in it was a set of car keys. "Got a pickup in the driveway. C'mon."

We hurried down the steps and climbed into a dirty, dusty vehicle. It was a '64 Chevy pickup with a V-8 engine and automatic transmission. We pulled out onto the roadway a few moments later. He hit the gas pedal hard and we jetted down the road toward town. A pair of fuzzy white dice dangled flimsily from the rear-view mirror. A little plastic man was mounted in the middle of the dashboard; his free-floating head bobbed up and down with each noticeable vibration.

The farmer glanced over and nodded his head at me. "I'm Henry…Henry Stockstead." He took his right hand off the wheel and held it toward me.

I reached for his hand. "Name's Kirby…" I started to reply, but Stockstead gasped and hit the brakes before I could finish my sentence.

A fish-man was standing in the middle of the road.

The tires screeched and the creature raised its arms. A split second before impact the creature hurtled to one side, but it was too late. The right fender caught it hard. There was a loud smacking noise and its body went spinning to the side. The pickup skidded to a stop a few yards down the road. Stockstead looked at me in astonishment.

"What in the love a' Mike was that thing?"

"It's been chasing me," I replied in a trembling voice. "I didn't think you'd help me if I told you the truth back at your door. I—I don't know what to tell you…but there's a bunch of 'em after me. Don't ask me what they are. All I know is they came up out of Graybill's pool and they've been chasing me all over the countryside. They already got another guy. He's dead…I think. My damn girlfriend's mixed up in this somehow…but I really don't know what the hell's going on." I stared Stockstead straight in the eye. "These are monsters…I mean *real* monsters. I think they came up out of Jacob's Pond." I glanced down the road and nodded my head. "And we better get out of here before anymore of them find us."

Stockstead looked like he'd just been kicked in the pants. "I gotta see this for myself." He popped open the glove compartment, fumbled around for a moment, then pulled out a flashlight.

"Come on," he said. We climbed out of the pickup. Stockstead grabbed a crowbar from under the driver's seat and we trotted back to the body. The overpowering stench stopped us a few feet away. Stockstead's face contorted with a look of nausea. "Damn...that thing stinks!"

We moved in closer and kneeled down beside it. Stockstead scanned it with his flashlight: no breathing, no twitching—there was no movement of any kind.

"I think it's dead," I said, my voice shivering.

Stockstead looked awestruck. "Well if that don't beat everything! Look at that thing will ya..." He glanced up at me and shook his head. "We gotta be dreamin'...this can't be real." He poked it in the ribs with the end of the crowbar.

It was then that everything really hit me. Stockstead, too, I think. This was a monster at our feet. A real, true-to-life monster. Not a dime novel, not a cheap horror movie, but a real, honest to goodness, slimy, grotesque, fish-like monster.

Stockstead looked at me contemplatingly. "They'll never believe us in town." He went back to the truck and grabbed an old blanket out of the back. "C'mon. Help me get this thing in the back of the pickup."

I cringed at the thought of touching it, but we wrapped the creature in the blanket and tossed it over the gate. We hopped back in and continued toward town. On the way down the road I started telling Stockstead about what had happened. We were almost to Graybill's when he pumped the breaks and slowed us to a crawl. "Good lord!" he exclaimed. He flicked on his brights; I looked down the road in the waning distance of the beams

Marching up the road was a bevy of lumbering fish-men.

"Turn around now! Get us out of here!" I yelled. Then Henry Stockstead did something that scared the hell out of me.

He punched it.

We went flying, straight down the road, straight for the approaching band of monsters. I scooted down in the seat and closed my eyes almost all the way. Henry had the Chevy up to about 50 when we zoomed into them. They went flying in all different directions. We didn't hit any of them, but we certainly sent them running for cover.

"Now *that's* how you play chicken!" Henry trumpeted loudly. He gave a war-whoop and hit off several blasts on the horn. I looked at him in disbelief.

"Way to go Henry!"

He took a hand off the wheel and shook his index finger. "That'll teach those goons to—"

An eruption of shattering glass cut off Stockstead in mid-sentence as the back window of the pickup exploded. A scaly hand shot through and wrapped itself over his mouth. The pickup swerved violently; I thought we were going to end up in the ditch. I leaned over and grabbed the wheel, trying to straighten us out. Suddenly a scaly hand clamped around my face, too. The stench was overpowering. I jerked forward violently and escaped its grasp but tumbled to the floorboard. Knowing we would crash at any second, I reached over and slammed on the brake pedal as hard as I could with both hands. Stockstead's feet were thrashing about wildly and almost kicked me in the head. I kept pressing down hard on the brake pedal; the pickup slowed to a stop.

I looked up and half-screamed.

The creature from the back of the pickup had revived and had thrust both hands around Stockstead's face, pulling his head back toward the jagged opening of the broken window. I could hear Stockstead's muffled screams blurting out between the webbed fingers of those scaly, monstrous hands. It looked as though his neck were about to snap. I glanced above Stockstead's head: there was a gun rack above the window—a shotgun lay across it.

I scrambled off the floor and went for the gun. As I grabbed the butt of it, one of the creature's hands came loose and smacked me hard across the face. I pitched backwards—along with the gun—and ended up back on the floorboard. The side of my head hit the radio, which came blaring to life. A rollicking country tune by Tex Ritter roared in at full volume, filling the cab with an outlandish sense of gaiety. Stockstead was still thrashing wildly about. The top of his head was being pulled into the jagged glass; blood trickled through his hair. I could see the creature's face just inches behind Stockstead's.

I raised the shotgun and aimed it through the broken window.

"Watch out, Henry!" I cried.

If Henry Stockstead was frightened by the hideous monster that was yanking at his head from behind, he was suddenly pale as the moon at the sight of a single gauge shotgun aiming inches past the side of his face. Only one of Henry's eyes was visible, and it went wide with terror.

I pulled the trigger.

A burst of buckshot went screaming past Stockstead's right ear, blasting straight into the creature's face. The impact sent it toppling backwards onto the bed of the pickup. It lay flat on its back, completely motionless. This time it was dead for sure.

I looked at Stockstead and shouted, "Are you okay?"

For a moment or two Stockstead was too shocked to say much of anything. He was holding his hand tightly over the right side of his face where a few pellets of buckshot had grazed into the flesh. I could see blood trickling slowing through his fingers and he grimaced widely in pain.

"What are you trying to do, buddy…blow my head off?"

"Sorry, Henry," I replied. "You're bleeding…"

"Hell yes I'm bleeding!" he shot back. "Is that thing dead?"

"I think so. C'mon…let's take a look."

We got out of the pickup and climbed into the back. The creature lay utterly still, its face completely blown off. I couldn't tell in the moonlight what color its blood was, but it looked as though it might be some dark shade of brown. I poked it in the ribs with the barrel of the shotgun—there was no reaction. I looked over at Stockstead.

"Got it for sure this time," I said.

It was then that I noticed how much Stockstead was really bleeding. Not only had the buckshot grazed him, but the creature's claw-like fingers had deeply punctured his skin in several places along both sides of his face and neck. There was also a considerable amount of blood oozing from the glass cuts on top of his head.  In short, he was a bloody mess.

He started to stagger so I grabbed him by the arm. "Gotta get you to a doctor…"

# CHAPTER SIX

I helped him climb down and into the passenger side of the pickup. I hopped behind the wheel, started the motor, and gunned it. We flew down the road toward the center of town. The police department was nearer than the hospital, so I headed in that direction. As we pulled up in front of the station I slammed on the brakes and laid on the horn. Two officers came running out a side door.

Stockstead managed to climb out of the pickup, but he was getting groggy from the loss of blood. He took a few staggering steps toward the approaching officers, then fell to the ground. Even though I had the catch of the century in the back of the pickup, my immediate thoughts were of Henry's wounds. I helped the officers carry him into an infirmary inside the station where a police medic began working on him.

"You're gonna be all right, Henry," I told him encouragingly.

I was pulled to the side by a couple of officers. They walked me down a hallway and into an office where they started to interrogate me. After a couple of minutes, a burly-looking, cigar-chomping sergeant named Riley burst through the door, demanding to know what had happened.

"What the hell's goin' on?" he trumpeted in a loud, demanding voice.

One of the officers pointed his finger at me. Riley moved in behind his desk, shooing a younger officer out of his chair. There was a noticeable creaking sound of wood being strained by too much weight as Riley settled his heavy frame into the chair. Then the interrogation started all over again.

"Let me get this straight," said Riley. He tipped his hat back, tapped his cigar, and pointed his pencil at the notes he had been scribbling, then in a skeptical tone he said, "You're telling me your girl friend…this, this Carrie Marshfield…along with her sister and a bunch of these…'fish-men'…as you've described them…attacked you and another guy out at Graybill's pool tonight. Is that right?"

"That's right."

"So…this Carrie and these fish-men chased after you…but you got away. Then you met up with this Stockstead fella who gave you a lift into town. On the way in you ran down one of these things and killed it…only it wasn't really dead…just faking or something. Then it smashed through the back window of the pickup and tried to kill Stockstead."

"That's right. That's when I shot it in the face."

Riley looked skeptically at the other officers in the room.

"With Stockstead's shotgun?" he asked.

"It's still lying in the back of the pickup out front."

"The shotgun?"

"No…the fish-man. Wanna see him?"

Riley looked at both officers and chomped on his cigar. "I can hardly wait."

We marched out of the station and gathered around the back end of the pickup. I thought Riley's eyes were going to pop out of his head. The cigar fell out of his mouth and two of the other officers staggered back several feet in horrified astonishment. I cringed myself, then looked the other way.

"Hell's bells!" Riley exploded. "What in heaven's name is that thing?"

The sight and stench of the dead creature was so overpowering that one of the officers turned away and threw up in the gutter. Riley looked at me in amazement; there was no longer any sense of doubt in his stare.

"Got a picture of this Carrie girl…in your wallet maybe?" he asked.

"No…but I've got one over at the apartment."

"Good. We'll pick it up on the way over to the pool."

Not long after, I was in a squad car racing over to my apartment. Riley drove; two other officers accompanied us. Behind us was another squad car with four more officers.

"Are you sure you don't have a picture of the sister?" Riley asked me.

"No…just Carrie. I took it through my front window when she was walking up to my door the other day…a Polaroid. I don't even think she saw me take it."

"Good. We'll pass it around to the rest of the boys for identification purposes. After that we'll head over to Graybill's and see what's happening there…then we'll check out the Marshfield house. I want you to stay put in your apartment for the time being. Barton here's gonna keep you company while we're gone. I want him to take a full report...don't leave anything out. We'll pick him up on the way back in." Riley looked over his shoulder at me, a stubby cigar hanging out of the side of his mouth. "This is the damnedest thing I've ever heard of."

We pulled up in front of my apartment a few minutes later, an old duplex over on Newell Street. It was 2 a.m. Riley waved for the officers in the other car to come inside as well. We all marched into my apartment. Turning the lights on, I motioned the officers into my living room.

"Wait here and I'll get the picture."

Riley followed me down the short hallway.

"You better change your clothes, Kirby. They stink to high heaven." Riley commented.

We opened the bedroom door and walked in. The stench seemed even greater as we stepped into the darkened room. I switched on the light.

"I missed you, Kirby."

Carrie stood against the back wall, still dressed in her wet swimsuit.

Riley pulled the cigar out of his mouth and pointed. "Is this her?"

Before I could answer, a powerful blow to the side of Riley's head sent him careening sideways into the wall. He collapsed in a heap next to my bed, unconscious. I whirled around and saw two fish-men standing behind me on either side. I started to cry out but was struck by a hard blow from the one nearest me, its slimy hand catching me flush on the temple. I crumpled to the floor, stunned. My head was spinning, but I tried to raise myself up. An instant later the things were all over me. In the other room police officers were screaming; there was the sound of a violent struggle. I heard one gunshot. Suddenly a hand pulled the hair on the back of my head and a cloth of foul smelling stuff was muzzled over my face. I blacked out completely.

# CHAPTER SEVEN

I don't know how much time passed, but when I woke up I was lying on a marble table, cold as ice, in a very dimly lit room. I could feel a wet, sticky substance running down the side of my cheek and a vile taste was in my mouth. Carrie was standing over me, holding a small glass of reddish solution that had been used to revive me.

"I'm glad you came out of it so quickly, Kirby. We haven't much time."

I didn't say anything at first. I was groggy, like when you first start to wake up in the morning—your eyes are still closed, you're still technically asleep, yet you have a conscious knowledge that you're still asleep; you can hear voices in the next room, even choose if you want to drift back into full sleep or wake up completely. That's how I felt on that cold marble slab. The only difference was that my eyes were wide open.

"Carrie..." I started to sit up but couldn't move. I raised my head up and saw the straps that were holding me down. I was so groggy it probably wouldn't have mattered.

I looked around. There was a window at the end of the room and a lamp on an old wooden stand near the wall. Another marble table lay parallel to me a few feet away. It was about eight feet long and had a wooden frame and wooden legs. Lying on the floor in-between though was something more ominous: a long, black oblong container—about the size of a coffin. I couldn't tell what it was made of, but it appeared to be quite solid. There was a seam about a foot above the floor that ran the length of it. Some type of mist appeared to be seeping out of it. In the middle, an inch or two above the seam, was a handle.

I spoke in a slurred manner, "Carrie, what the hell is going on?"

She put her finger to my lips "Quiet, my love."

My eyes rolled in my sockets as my head lowered back onto the table. "What happened to Vince? Where's Helen?" I asked groggily.

"Vince is fine. Helen will be with us soon."

"But what happened?" My voice rose a little as I raised my head and shoulders up again. "What were those damn things chasing me?"

"Shhh!" Carrie scolded me softly. She pushed gently and lowered my head and shoulders back down.

I had to be dreaming. It was like a dream, yet I knew it wasn't.

Carrie stroked her hand on my cheek. "You were special to me, Kirby...not like the others. The others were needed for the ritual of the flesh...the metamorphosis that allows our continued crossover into the surface world. It's something Helen and I must go through every ten years. Our mother was..." She hesitated for a moment, as though changing her mind about telling me anything further.

"You murdered Vince," I said.

"You're wrong, Kirby. Vince is alive. He and the others will soon take their place as helots for the great master...the great master from below the sea. But you..." The slightest trace of a smile crossed her face. "You'll be with me. I'm allowed it."

"You're completely nuts," I garbled. "The police...they know about you."

"The ones at your apartment are dead or unconscious. We'll be long gone before they recover or others discover what's happened to them."

"Gone...where?"

"Your contact with the police means time is short. We'll be leaving soon...returning to..." She hesitated and looked away, then said, "You'll be coming with us."

"Coming where?"

Before she could answer, I heard a door open. Walking into the room was a tall older man whom I recognized as Carrie's father—so much for grisly cannery accidents. He was dressed completely in black and his face was hidden by a scraggly beard and mustache. A stench followed him into the room. I looked up and saw four fish-men straggle in behind him. Even in my grogginess I started to tremble. My eyes widened as they followed the misshapen creatures across the room.

Homer Marshfield stopped at the end of the long black container. He signaled to the fish-men and spoke in a strange tongue. All four of them shambled over to the container. One of them grabbed the handle and pulled up. The container opened up at the seam, just like a coffin. Within it was a strange mold made out of some type of opaque stone.

The mold was in the shape of a man.

I could see a waft of mist rising from within. The fish-men positioned themselves in pairs at either end. Then they stooped over and grabbed something from within and began to lift. It appeared to be another fish-man, only this one was dripping with some type of horrendous ectoplasm that fell to the floor in large, quivering droplets. They carried him over and placed him on the other marble table. When they moved away I got a good look at it as it lay motionless on the table.

Then I started to scream.

I screamed long and loud. I kept on screaming. Carrie rushed over and tried to calm me. I screamed even louder. A look of disdain came over the face of Homer Marshfield. He barked another command in that strange tongue and the four fish-men began moving toward me. I went silent, staring up at the approaching figures in utter horror. They positioned themselves around me, each one grabbing an arm or leg.

Homer Marshfield then began untying my straps.

Even in my dizzy state I tried to struggle. I riggled my arms and legs as much as I could, but it was hopeless. The fish-men held on tight.

So I started screaming again.

Carrie was standing next to me the whole time, trying to calm me. I felt the straps slide off as the fish-men began to lift me up. I started kicking again, harder than before. My screams were ear piercing. My mind was reeling in a frenzy of total panic. Then through the wave of my own screams came a sound in the distance.

It was a gunshot.

Carrie and her father glanced up, expressions of surprised concern on their faces. Homer Marshfield barked another command and the fish-men laid me back on the table. The sound of a violent commotion erupted from somewhere downstairs. The police had obviously arrived sooner than expected. Numerous gunshots followed and I could hear glass breaking and wood splintering. Yelling and screaming echoed through the floorboards, along with that awful baying sound emitted from the throats of fish-men below.

Homer Marshfield looked down at me, a look of rage on his face.

"We'll deal with you momentarily, my friend," he said, leaning over directly into my face.

A look of concern came over Carrie's face when she heard this.

"Father, you promised."

"We've no time for anything further—and he can't be left alive."

Homer pointed to me and signaled to the four fish-men. They began lumbering toward me.

At this Carrie moved quickly between my table and the advancing monsters. She uttered a guttural command to them and they stopped momentarily, looking back at Homer as though confused.

"You'll not harm him, father," she said firmly. "On my life you will not harm him."

A look of disdained resignation came over Homer Marshfield's face.

"Very well...daughter. But we must leave...*now*."

He turned and walked briskly from the room, the four fish-men sauntering apishly after him, two of them carrying the fish-man from the table. Carrie remained in the room with me. She stared down at me with a look of strange intensity on her face.

"Kirby…you'll never know the wonder of it. Another world…another life." I thought I saw tears welling up in her eyes. Then she did something I'll never forget.

She bent over and kissed me.

I was repulsed, yet strangely taken by it. For a moment we were back at my apartment. The passionate nights…the memories of her touch. She pulled away and looked at me one last time. Then she was gone.

I was alone in the room

I must have lain there for at least a minute or two. I tried sitting up, but my head began to swim so I laid back down. Finally, I flopped my legs over the side of the table. I managed to pull myself to my feet and struggle to the window. The stench in that oppressed room was almost overpowering. I turned the latch and swung the window outward. Fresh air poured in rich and sweet and helped revive me a little. I looked outward. I was on the third floor, looking toward the east. As I gazed over the illuminated countryside, I could make out the vague outline of the Blue Mountains in the distance. Its slopes were dotted with the pinpoint lights of farmhouses and cars moving along the various county roads that criss-crossed the countryside. Nearest to me I could see the large clump of Chestnut trees that I had hidden in earlier. Beyond that I could see the light of the moon reflecting off of Jacob's Pond. There were still a number of fish-men around it; they appeared to be diving in, one by one.

The commotion had gotten louder downstairs; gunshots continued to ring out above the din of yelling and screaming. Some of the noise came from, I thought, outside the house, maybe from the driveway area or perhaps from around front. I even thought I heard the sound of gunshots coming from the direction of Graybill's pool, but I couldn't be certain. Then I saw a figure emerge from the far side of the clump of Chestnut trees.

It was Carrie.

Even in the pale moonlight I couldn't mistake her. She ran straight for Jacob's Pond. I saw her sleek figure duck under the barbed wire fence and trot up to the edge of the water. Then for just a moment she turned and gazed back toward the house. I'll never be certain, but I could swear she was looking back at me as I hung out of the upper window of that awful house—staring at me with those almond eyes. A moment later she turned and dove into the dark water. She did not re-emerge.

The nature of my thoughts was weary, confused, and groggy as I hung out that window gazing into the half-darkness. There were flashlights now, emerging from the far side of the trees as the police chased a number of straggling fish-men toward the pond. Presently I detected sounds behind me—voices and footsteps. My ears were assailed by the sound of splintering wood, then the door burst open and five gun-wielding policemen rushed into the room. Two of them leveled their guns directly at me.

"Hit the deck...now!"

I dropped to the floor—probably the easiest thing I had done all night—and muttered a few words into the floorboards, telling them who I was. I could hear guns sliding back into their holsters and suddenly I was being helped up and led out of the room. As they took me downstairs I saw the bodies of fish-men strewn everywhere. There were wounded policemen, too, being tended to by other officers. Some of them were weeping from agony, some from fright. They got me outside and walked me slowly out to the roadway where a number of patrol cars were parked.

Then I did the conventional thing and fainted.

## CHAPTER EIGHT

I woke up the next day in a hospital bed, recovering from the effects of the strange drug I had been subjected to. I was on my feet later in the evening and released the next day. I spent most of my time over the next few days with the local police and the FBI.

"Where's Carrie?" I asked one of the agents during one of my numerous interrogations.

"We'll have to get back to you on that," he answered elusively.

But I never found out what happened to Carrie Marshfield. The same for her sister and father, and for that matter, what they did with all the bodies of the fish-men that had been killed. I did hear that Riley and most of the other officers had survived the ambush at my apartment. They had been subjected to the same drug that was used on me and were out for hours. None of them were the worse for wear other than a few side effects—nausea and prolonged vomiting. Henry Stockstead, too, made it through with flying colors. I still see Henry occasionally, but we seldom speak of our incident. We're not allowed to. The FBI made sure of that. Oh sure, they paid us a lot of money for our silence and cooperation—can't have the country go into a tizzy over the greatest, most horrifying scientific discovery of modern times. So we perpetually bite our tongues and keep the whole thing to ourselves. I don't understand how they managed to keep it so quiet with all the police officers involved—but that's the FBI for you.

They never did reopen Graybill's pool. A day or two after the incident, a story was leaked out about how the pool wasn't up to local health and safety standards. It's doors never reopened to the public. The dressing rooms and concession stand were torn down long ago, but most of the pool is still there. You can see it to this day, lying behind a wooden fence at the corner of Reser and Kendall roads just outside the Walla Walla city limits. Jacob's pond was drained, as best they could, and a short time later was covered with a huge cement slab, courtesy of the Army Corps of Engineers.

Is Carrie Marshfield still alive? Was she even human? I don't know—I don't want to know; because I know what it was that Carrie and her "family" had in store for me that night. In fact, I know the horrible truth about all the other young men who disappeared mysteriously over that long, terrible summer. You see we were all bachelors with little or no family. No one to check up on us. No one to miss us. During that ghastly night as I lay helpless inside the upper floor of the Marshfield house, I saw the horrible truth lying on the marble table next to me. I shudder at the memory of it. As I lay there in a groggy haze, I screamed at the sight of the fish-man lying on that marble slab just inches away from me; but it wasn't the sight of a fish-man that had frightened me, but rather, the sight of *this* fish-man. He lay staring at me in all his hideous repulsiveness: webbed, claw-like fingers, scaly dark green skin, a bloated white belly, and a slimy putrescence over his entire carcass. But none of that had made me scream. What shook me to the inner depth of my soul was its pitiful face and those terrified, saddened eyes. For staring at me wasn't the face of a horrendous monster...

*but the agonized face of Vince Locatti.*

## THE END

*If you've enjoyed this book, you will not want to miss these terrific titles…*

## ARMCHAIR SCI-FI, FANTASY, & HORROR DOUBLE NOVELS, $12.95 each

**D-1**     **THE GALAXY RAIDERS** by William P. McGivern
             **SPACE STATION #1** by Frank Belknap Long

**D-2**     **THE PROGRAMMED PEOPLE** by Jack Sharkey
             **SLAVES OF THE CRYSTAL BRAIN** by William Carter Sawtelle

**D-3**     **YOU'RE ALL ALONE** by Fritz Leiber
             **THE LIQUID MAN** by Bernard C. Gilford

**D-4**     **CITADEL OF THE STAR LORDS** by Edmund Hamilton
             **VOYAGE TO ETERNITY** by Milton Lesser

**D-5**     **IRON MEN OF VENUS** by Don Wilcox
             **THE MAN WITH ABSOLUTE MOTION** by Noel Loomis

**D-6**     **WHO SOWS THE WIND...** by Rog Phillips
             **THE PUZZLE PLANET** by Robert A. W. Lowndes

**D-7**     **PLANET OF DREAD** by Murray Leinster
             **TWICE UPON A TIME** by Charles L. Fontenay

**D-8**     **THE TERROR OUT OF SPACE** by Dwight V. Swain
             **QUEST OF THE GOLDEN APE** by Ivar Jorgensen and Adam Chase

**D-9**     **SECRET OF MARRACOTT DEEP** by Henry Slesar
             **PAWN OF THE BLACK FLEET** by Mark Clifton.

**D-10**     **BEYOND THE RINGS OF SATURN** by Robert Moore Williams
             **A MAN OBSESSED** by Alan E. Nourse

## ARMCHAIR SCIENCE FICTION CLASSICS, $12.95 each

**C-1**     **THE GREEN MAN**
             by Harold M. Sherman

**C-2**     **A TRACE OF MEMORY**
             By Keith Laumer

**C-3**     **INTO PLUTONIAN DEPTHS**
             by Stanton A. Coblentz

## ARMCHAIR MASTERS OF SCIENCE FICTION SERIES, $16.95 each

**M-1**     **MASTERS OF SCIENCE FICTION, Vol. One**
             Bryce Walton—"Dark of the Moon" and other tales

**M-2**     **MASTERS OF SCIENCE FICTION, Vol. Two**
             Jerome Bixby: "One Way Street" and other tales

*If you've enjoyed this book, you will not want to miss these terrific titles…*

## ARMCHAIR SCI-FI & HORROR DOUBLE NOVELS, $12.95 each

**D-11**  **PERIL OF THE STARMEN** by Kris Neville
**THE STRANGE INVASION** by Murray Leinster

**D-12**  **THE STAR LORD** by Boyd Ellanby
**CAPTIVES OF THE FLAME** by Samuel R. Delany

**D-13**  **MEN OF THE MORNING STAR** by Edmund Hamilton
**PLANET FOR PLUNDER** by Hal Clement and Sam Merwin, Jr.

**D-14**  **ICE CITY OF THE GORGON** by Chester S. Geier and Richard Shaver
**WHEN THE WORLD TOTTERED** by Lester del Rey

**D-15**  **WORLDS WITHOUT END** by Clifford D. Simak
**THE LAVENDER VINE OF DEATH** by Don Wilcox

**D-16**  **SHADOW ON THE MOON** by Joe Gibson
**ARMAGEDDON EARTH** by Geoff St. Reynard

**D-17**  **THE GIRL WHO LOVED DEATH** by Paul W. Fairman
**SLAVE PLANET** by Laurence M. Janifer

**D-18**  **SECOND CHANCE** by J. F. Bone
**MISSION TO A DISTANT STAR** by Frank Belknap Long

**D-19**  **THE SYNDIC** by C. M. Kornbluth
**FLIGHT TO FOREVER** by Poul Anderson

**D-20**  **SOMEWHERE I'LL FIND YOU** by Milton Lesser
**THE TIME ARMADA** by Fox B. Holden

## ARMCHAIR SCIENCE FICTION CLASSICS, $12.95 each

**C-4**  **CORPUS EARTHLING**
by Louis Charbonneau

**C-5**  **THE TIME DISSOLVER**
by Jerry Sohl

**C-6**  **WEST OF THE SUN**
by Edgar Pangborn

## ARMCHAIR SCIENCE FICTION & HORROR GEMS SERIES, $12.95 each

**G-1**  **SCIENCE FICTION GEMS, Vol. One**
Isaac Asimov and others

**G-2**  **HORROR GEMS, Vol. One**
Carl Jacobi and others

*If you've enjoyed this book, you will not want to miss these terrific titles...*

## ARMCHAIR SCI-FI & HORROR DOUBLE NOVELS, $12.95 each

**D-31**    **A HOAX IN TIME** by Keith Laumer
**INSIDE EARTH** by Poul Anderson

**D-32**    **TERROR STATION** by Dwight V. Swain
**THE WEAPON FROM ETERNITY** by Dwight V. Swain

**D-33**    **THE SHIP FROM INFINITY** by Edmond Hamilton
**TAKEOFF** by C. M. Kornbluth

**D-34**    **THE METAL DOOM** by David H. Keller
**TWELVE TIMES ZERO** by Howard Browne

**D-35**    **HUNTERS OUT OF SPACE** by Joseph Kelleam
**INVASION FROM THE DEEP** by Paul W. Fairman,

**D-36**    **THE BEES OF DEATH** by Robert Moore Williams
**A PLAGUE OF PYTHONS** by Frederick Pohl

**D-37**    **THE LORDS OF QUARMALL** by Fritz Leiber and Harry Fischer
**BEACON TO ELSEWHERE** by James H. Schmitz

**D-38**    **BEYOND PLUTO** by John S. Campbell
**ARTERY OF FIRE** by Thomas N. Scortia

**D-39**    **SPECIAL DELIVERY** by Kris Neville
**NO TIME FOR TOFFEE** by Charles F. Meyers

**D-40**    **JUNGLE IN THE SKY** by Milton Lesser
**RECALLED TO LIFE** by Robert Silverberg

## ARMCHAIR SCIENCE FICTION CLASSICS, $12.95 each

**C-10**    **MARS IS MY DESTINATION**
by Frank Belknap Long

**C-11**    **SPACE PLAGUE**
by George O. Smith

**C-12**    **SO SHALL YE REAP**
by Rog Phillips

## ARMCHAIR SCIENCE FICTION & HORROR GEMS SERIES, $12.95 each

**G-3**    **SCIENCE FICTION GEMS, Vol. Two**
James Blish and others

**G-4**    **HORROR GEMS, Vol. Two**
Joseph Payne Brennan and others

*If you've enjoyed this book, you will not want to miss these terrific titles...*

## ARMCHAIR SCI-FI, FANTASY, & HORROR DOUBLE NOVELS, $12.95 each

**D-41**  **FULL CYCLE** by Clifford D. Simak
**IT WAS THE DAY OF THE ROBOT** by Frank Belknap Long

**D-42**  **THIS CROWDED EARTH** by Robert Bloch
**REIGN OF THE TELEPUPPETS** by Daniel Galouye

**D-43**  **THE CRISPIN AFFAIR** by Jack Sharkey
**THE RED HELL OF JUPITER** by Paul Ernst

**D-44**  **PLANET OF DREAD** by Dwight V. Swain
**WE THE MACHINE** by Gerald Vance

**D-45**  **THE STAR HUNTER** by Edmond Hamilton
**THE ALIEN** by Raymond F. Jones

**D-46**  **WORLD OF IF** by Rog Phillips
**SLAVE RAIDERS FROM MERCURY** by Don Wilcox

**D-47**  **THE ULTIMATE PERIL** by Robert Abernathy
**PLANET OF SHAME** by Bruce Elliot

**D-48**  **THE FLYING EYES** by J. Hunter Holly
**SOME FABULOUS YONDER** by Phillip Jose Farmer

**D-49**  **THE COSMIC BUNGLERS** by Geoff St. Reynard
**THE BUTTONED SKY** by Geoff St. Reynard

**D-50**  **TYRANTS OF TIME** by Milton Lesser
**PARIAH PLANET** by Murray Leinster

## ARMCHAIR SCIENCE FICTION CLASSICS, $12.95 each

**C-13**  **SUNKEN WORLD**
by Stanton A. Coblentz

**C-14**  **THE LAST VIAL**
by Sam McClatchie, M. D.

**C-15**  **WE WHO SURVIVED (THE FIFTH ICE AGE)**
by Sterling Noel

## ARMCHAIR MASTERS OF SCIENCE FICTION SERIES, $16.95 each

**MS-5**  **MASTERS OF SCIENCE FICTION, Vol. Five**
Winston K. Marks—Test Colony and other tales

**MS-6**  **MASTERS OF SCIENCE FICTION, Vol. Six**
Fritz Leiber—Deadly Moon and other tales

*If you've enjoyed this book, you will not want to miss these terrific titles...*

## ARMCHAIR SCI-FI & HORROR DOUBLE NOVELS, $12.95 each

**D-51**    **A GOD NAMED SMITH** by Henry Slesar
**WORLDS OF THE IMPERIUM** by Keith Laumer

**D-52**    **CRAIG'S BOOK** by Don Wilcox
**EDGE OF THE KNIFE** by H. Beam Piper

**D-53**    **THE SHINING CITY** by Rena M. Vale
**THE RED PLANET** by Russ Winterbotham

**D-54**    **THE MAN WHO LIVED TWICE** by Rog Phillips
**VALLEY OF THE CROEN** by Lee Tarbell

**D-55**    **OPERATION DISASTER** by Milton Lesser
**LAND OF THE DAMNED** by Berkeley Livingston

**D-56**    **CAPTIVE OF THE CENTAURIANESS** by Poul Anderson
**A PRINCESS OF MARS** by Edgar Rice Burroughs

**D-57**    **THE NON-STATISTICAL MAN** by Raymond F. Jones
**MISSION FROM MARS** by Rick Conroy

**D-58**    **INTRUDERS FROM THE STARS** by Ross Rocklynne
**FLIGHT OF THE STARLING** by Chester S. Geier

**D-59**    **COSMIC SABOTEUR** by Frank M. Robinson
**LOOK TO THE STARS** by Willard Hawkins

**D-60**    **THE MOON IS HELL!** by John W. Campbell, Jr.
**THE GREEN WORLD** by Hal Clement

## ARMCHAIR SCIENCE FICTION CLASSICS, $12.95 each

**C-16**    **THE SHAVER MYSTERY, Book Three**
by Richard S. Shaver

**C-17**    **THE PLANET STRAPPERS**
by Raymond Z. Gallun

**C-18**    **THE FOURTH "R"**
by George O. Smith

## ARMCHAIR SCIENCE FICTION & HORROR GEMS SERIES, $12.95 each

**G-5**    **SCIENCE FICTION GEMS, Vol. Three**
C. M. Kornbluth and others

**G-6**    **HORROR GEMS, Vol. Three**
August Derleth and others

*If you've enjoyed this book, you will not want to miss these terrific titles…*

## ARMCHAIR SCI-FI & HORROR DOUBLE NOVELS, $12.95 each

## ARMCHAIR SCIENCE FICTION & FANTASY CLASSICS, $12.95 each

# CREATURES FROM THE DARKNESS...

*It was odd that a big city newspaper like the Chicago Globe would send out two of its best reporters to investigate a hen house slaughter and the mysterious appearance of a naked man in a farmer's field.  Nevertheless, Don Reed and Nita Ayer were sent packing to the wilds of Wisconsin to cover the story. Upon their arrival they found a farmer who was hesitant to talk—seemingly afraid of someone or some thing.  Then at the local jail there was the strange 19-year old who couldn't even speak English, who didn't have a stitch of clothing to his name, who seemed to want to stay in jail.  But when the youth turned up dead, the story took a horrifying turn into the unknown.  Soon, out of the darkness of the night came an unbelievable man with a crystal; and out of that same darkness came a terrifying power…*

# CAST OF CHARACTERS

### DON REED
*He was investigating an odd story—a nude man in a farmer's field—but the more he investigated, the more dangerous it got.*

### NITA AYER
*Another crack reporter. Her thirst for solving mysteries perhaps went further than her job description required.*

### PROFESSOR HARKER
*He claimed to know the truth about the story that Reed and Ayer were investigating. But how much did he really know?*

### MERTHU
*Who was he? He was a jail inmate who owned no clothes, couldn't speak English, and didn't even know how to eat!*

### SAMADU
*This giant of a man was the mysterious servant of a mysterious man within the confines of a most mysterious house.*

### JOHN McCLOY
*He found a naked man in his field one morning, but he knew there was something far more mysterious than nudity afoot.*

### CLANNING
*This small town sheriff was faced with a pretty tough decision—which big city reporter to arrest for murder!*

# TO WATCH
# BY NIGHT

By
ROBERT MOORE WILLIAMS

ARMCHAIR FICTION
PO Box 4369, Medford, Oregon   97501-0168

*For more information about Armchair Books and products, visit our
website at…*

**www.armchairfiction.com**

*Or email us at…*

**armchairfiction@yahoo.com**

# CHAPTER ONE
*The Ghostly Assassin*

"FOR CRIPE'S sake, lady, look out!" Don Reed shouted in horror. "He's going to shoot you!"

The girl, clad in a yellow linen dress that revealed shapely legs and hips, was half a block ahead of Don Reed. She was walking in the same direction he was going and he had already noticed her. He had also seen the man sneaking up behind her but he had paid no particular attention to either of them until the man had suddenly pulled a gun out of his pocket and had taken hasty aim at the back of the girl in the yellow dress.

It was mid morning and there were only a few shoppers on the street. Cars were crawling by on the asphalt, the drivers exercising tender care for their tires. On the corner a newsboy who had made himself hoarse with joy was shouting, "Another Japanese battleship sunk. Read all abooout it!"

All in all, it was a perfectly normal morning in Chicago, except that cold-blooded murder was about to be committed on one of the Loop's side streets.

Don Reed was half a block away, too far to do anything except shout. He yelled at the top of his lungs, *"Look out!"* His voice was loud enough even to drown out the newsboy.

Startled pedestrians turned to gape at him. The killer jerked up the gun. The girl in the yellow dress seemed to hear him. She ducked.

Boom!

The sharp spiteful crack of the pistol echoed through the city streets.

The girl in the yellow dress kept on ducking. She turned half way around and Reed caught one glimpse of her face. She ducked out of sight.

One second she was on the sidewalk, an extremely frightened girl trying to dodge the bullet of an assassin. The next second she was gone.

The killer stood without moving a muscle. If some super-magician had turned him into a stone statue, the statue would have shown no more ability to move than did the man with the gun. He seemed to be frozen to the spot.

Then, as the girl had done, he vanished.

One instant a girl in a yellow dress was standing on the sidewalk and a man with a smoking gun in his hand was standing behind her. The next instant both the girl and the killer had vanished.

DON REED was running toward them when they went out of seeing. Abruptly he stopped. Without realizing he was doing it, he put his back against the nearest solid wall and stood there, gazing from slitted eyes at what was happening on the street.

The cars on the asphalt were veering to a halt, their wide-eyed drivers staring at the sidewalk. Pedestrians were standing without moving. In front of Reed a fat woman suddenly squawked, took three short steps, and abruptly sat down. She began to scream at the top of her voice. A man was leaning against a lamppost vigorously blowing his nose. He would blow his nose, put his handkerchief in his pocket, then jerk the handkerchief out and blow his nose again. A woman with two children aged about six and nine years was walking rapidly away. "You get right away from here, Johnny and Mary," she was saying. "You get right away from here."

A cop came running up. "What's going on here?" he vigorously demanded. "I heard a gun go off. Who got shot?"

The newsboy at the corner had seen everything. "It was two ghosts," he whispered. "One ghost took a shot at another ghost and they both vanished into thin air."

The cop glared at him.

"Into thin air," the boy repeated. "I was lookin' right at 'em. Before I could bat my eyes, they were gone."

"You get to hell back to selling newspapers!" the cop said. He turned to the fat woman sitting on the sidewalk. "What happened, Madam?" he said.

She shook her head and continued screaming.

The cop walked over to the man leaning against the lamppost. "What the hell is going on around here?" he demanded.

The man vigorously blew his nose. "I'm going home," he said firmly. "When I get there I'm going to lie down and rest. I feel faint." Turning away from the officer, he walked down the street. The farther he walked, the faster he went. By the time he reached the corner he was running.

The baffled officer walked over to Reed.

DON REED was as hard-boiled a newspaperman as had ever covered the police run. He had started his newspaper career working for a news bureau, learning the trade the hard way, and he was now one of the two star reporters on the Chicago *Globe*. He was tall and wiry, and while a grin came easily to his face, he usually talked like something that had walked straight out of *The Front Page*. He believed little that he saw with his own eyes, nothing that he heard, and nothing that he read in the papers unless he had written it himself, in which case he knew how big a percentage of truth it contained. He had not moved from the wall.

"Do you believe in ghosts?" he said in answer to the cop's question.

"Do I—" The officer choked and began to get red in the face.

"I thought you didn't," Reed sighed. "You don't look like a man who believed in ghosts."

"What's ghosts got to do with that shot I heard?" the patrolman demanded.

"Did you hear a shot?" Reed inquired.

"I certainly did."

"You did? Ah, well, I thought I did too, but it is very easy to be mistaken in matters like this," Reed answered. "Now, officer, if you will excuse me, I have work to do."

"Hey, what about that shot?"

"It must have been a back-fire," the reporter threw back over his shoulder. On the sidewalk near the spot where the killer had stood a small object was lying. Reed picked it up, glanced at it, swiftly thrust it into his pocket and continued on his way.

It was an empty pistol cartridge. The murderer had been using an automatic. When he had fired the gun, the empty cartridge case had been ejected.

Reed wanted two things, one of them immediately. He entered the nearest bar. "Rye," he said to the bartender. "A shot of rye, straight."

He downed the liquor with a gulp. It warmed his stomach, took away a little of the cold feeling of tension that had come over him. He wasn't scared. A reporter develops a sang-froid carelessness that enables him to view sudden death with detachment. But Reed was terribly startled.

He had seen a man shoot at a girl.

This could happen. Men usually didn't shoot women but it had been done. There was nothing new in it.

He had seen the girl vanish.

This couldn't happen.

But it had happened, right before his eyes! Reed's first wild thought was that he had been tricked by some kind of an illusion. He had once seen an elephant vanish, before the eyes of a startled and thrilled audience, at the wave of a magician's wand. But that had happened on the stage. The girl had vanished on the street.

There remained the possibility that he had been the victim of a hallucination. In that case, the fat woman, the newsboy, and the man with the yen for blowing his nose, had suddenly been afflicted with the same hallucination, which was illogical.

If illusion and hallucination were ruled out, only one possibility was left: that the girl, along with the man who had tried to kill her, had actually vanished. She hadn't ducked into a store; she hadn't dodged across the street; she hadn't run around the block. He had been looking right at her and she had ducked from sight in the split fraction of a second.

Reed fretfully ordered another rye. "Do you believe in ghosts?" he asked the bartender.

The bartender was a large man with a placid face. He was not startled at the question but he did seem to think it called for mature consideration. "Well," he began, "there is some that do, and some that don't. As for me, I can't say whether I do or whether I don't."

"Thank you," said Reed, leaving the saloon.

A drink had been the first thing he had wanted, a drink and a chance to think. There still remained the second thing.

He thought, when the girl in the yellow dress had turned around, that he had recognized her. He thought she was Nita Ayer.

The second thing he wanted to do was to go see Nita.

THERE were two star reporters on staff of the *Globe*. Don Reed was one. Nita Ayer was the second.

He found her in her cubbyhole off the newsroom. As he entered she looked up at him and smiled.

"Hello, Don," she said. "What's new today."

She was wearing a yellow dress.

Reed sat down on the corner of her desk. "Did anyone ever tell you that you are beautiful?" he said.

A smile danced in the depths of her dark eyes. "Frequently," she gaily answered. "Men often stop me on the street just to tell me I'm beautiful, artists want to paint me, and photographers try to take candid camera shots of me. I also endorse things. Nita Ayer, world famous beauty and newspaper woman, smokes this brand of cigarettes. Nita Ayer eats this brand of breakfast food. Nita Ayer wears the famous Kant-Rip swimsuit. Of course, Don, I've been told I'm beautiful. Hundreds of times." She paused and looked impishly at him. "But I'm always glad to hear it again."

Reed grinned at her. "When are you going to marry me?" he said.

She looked startled. "Don!" she gasped, performing a rapid calculation on her fingers. "This is Thursday. You don't ever propose to me on Thursdays. You propose to me regularly on Saturday nights and Monday mornings—"

"Because I have money on Saturday night and I want you to help me spend it. On Monday morning I have a hangover and I want you to hold my head," Reed gravely explained.

"Go away!" she said, in mock rage. "You've broken my girlish heart. Here I thought you loved me for myself alone and now I find it's only because you want me to help spend your filthy money or to hold your tousled head. Get thee from me, villain. I have work to do."

She turned back to her battered typewriter and resumed work on the story she was writing. She used the hunt and peck system in operating the typewriter. Reed watched her in silence. They gray moonstone in the bracelet she wore on her left arm winked at him as she operated the typewriter. He read the story she was writing.

"Six months you have been working on this newspaper and you still do not know how to spell 'negotiations'," he observed.

"Oh, dear!" she said.

He told her how to spell the word and she crossed out the error and wrote it in correctly.

"Where did you live before you came here to work?" he questioned quietly.

She glanced quickly up at him, then down again, a quick measuring look. "Is that a question for a quiz program? I came from New York."

"Where did you live in New York?" Reed continued.

"In Brooklyn," she quickly answered.

"Brooklyn is not in New York," Reed corrected.

"Isn't it? I mean…of course it isn't.

I usually say I lived in New York because most people out here think Brooklyn is a part of New York." She lit a cigarette and looked keenly at him through the smoke.

"You don't talk like an inhabitant of Brooklyn," Reed observed.

"Do they talk in a special way?" she asked.

REED sighed inwardly. In spite of the fact that he had been almost daily in the company of this girl ever since she had turned up and had promptly been given a job on the *Globe*, he did not know her background. She had told him she had come from New York and that had been enough for him until now. All he knew about her was what his eyes told him, that she was beautiful, that she had a remarkable talent for gathering news, that she was quick-witted and very intelligent. When she had come to work, he, and every unattached male on the staff, had promptly fallen in love with her. It had been a delicious, delightful game. Now it was something else. When he tried to think of what else it might be, he had to fight the cold chills that passed up and down his spine.

"Do you believe in ghosts?" he said irrelevantly.

For a second a mask dropped over her face. Her gaze, fixed on him; it was hard and mercilessly measuring in its intensity. Then she laughed.

"Of course!" she said, snubbing her half-smoked cigarette. "I believe in ghosts and fairies and werewolves and vampires. Except the green ones. I don't believe in green vampires. They're too utterly ridiculous. A vampire just has to be gray. Don't you think so?"

The glint of a smile was in her eyes and there was gay nonsense in her laughter.

"Don't laugh!" the reporter said harshly. "I'm talking seriously now. Do you believe in ghosts?"

"Why, Don..." Surprise was in her voice. "What on earth is the matter with you? Have you gone wacky on me, or something?"

"I think I have," Reed answered. "But tell me this: How long have you been in the office?"

"Possibly thirty minutes," she answered. "Don...what's this all about?"

"I'm practicing for a bout with the Quiz Kids," Reed said. He reached into his pocket, took out the empty cartridge case and laid it on the desk in front of her.

"Do you know what that is?" he challenged.

She glanced from the reporter to the piece of brass. A puzzled frown wrinkled the smooth skin of her forehead. "It goes in a gun, doesn't it?" she said. "I don't know much about guns but I was in a shooting gallery once and the things that came out of the guns looked like this, except they were smaller. Is it—is it—do they call them shells? Or cartridges? Which is it?" She glanced lightly up at Reed.

"When placed in a gun and fired at a human, the prosecuting attorney usually labels them exhibit B, the cartridge from the murder weapon," the reporter answered. "What I want to know is, was this cartridge fired at you within the past thirty minutes?"

"At me!" she squealed in fright. "Did somebody try to kill me?" Then her face changed. She looked suspiciously at the reporter. "What's the gag, Don?" she said. "Don't keep me waiting. I'm *dying* of suspense."

THERE was ice in Don Reed's eyes, and something more than ice, a trace of panicky fear that he was fighting to keep under control. But when he spoke his voice was calm and suave; it gave no hint of the emotional storm within his mind. "Nita," he said, "the stage lost a great actress when you decided to become a newspaper woman. You might have been a very great actress, one of the best."

"Thank you, Don," she said. And now, for the first time, a trace of panic showed in the tones of her voice.

"Nita," Reed said slowly. "I'm your friend. You know that, don't you?"

"Yes, Don." She had recovered her composure.

"I love you, Nita," the reporter said simply.

"I—I'm afraid I know that too," she said hastily. Again her composure slipped.

"I would do anything I could for you," Reed continued. "You know that too, don't you?"

"Y—yes."

Reed's eyes drilled into her. "Then why are you lying to me?" he snapped.

"Me?" she gasped, "I'm lying—"

"Quit stalling!" Reed said harshly. "You're in trouble and I know it and I want to help you if I can."

He knew, as he watched her reaction, that he had been right in saying she was a great actress. Her face showed surprise and bewilderment and a lack of understanding, but there was no hint that she knew what he was talking about.

"Stalling?" she whispered, bewilderment in her voice. "Don, I can't even begin—"

"Quit it!" he snapped.

"But Don—"

"Look at the collar of your dress," Reed rasped. "There's a groove in your dress collar where the slug that came out of this cartridge missed you by the skin of your teeth. If you aren't the girl in the yellow dress whom I saw vanish, then how did you get that bullet hole in your collar?"

The minute he had entered the room, Reed had seen the groove left by the bullet. It was at the side of her neck and was located in such a position that she could not see it except by pulling the collar out and even then she would need a mirror to see the mark. Obviously she did not know it was there and Reed had had no intention of calling it to her attention except as a last resort.

He knew she was stalling. He knew she was lying, pretending, acting. Beyond the shadow of a doubt he knew that Nita Ayer was the girl in the yellow dress who had almost been murdered and had vanished from sight like smoke before the wind.

Every time he thought of it, cold chills went up his spine. This girl who sat across the desk from him, Nita Ayer, was able to vanish, to disappear, to slide away into nothingness!

Who was Nita Ayer? *What* was she?

When he spoke, her face went dead white. She jerked her head around and down, trying to see the mark on her dress. When she could not see the groove that way, she snatched at the collar, pulled it out and around. Her fingers touched the spot where the frayed, broken threads marked the passage of the bullet.

REED waited for her to react. What would she say now? What would she *do?* She could not deny the presence of the bullet mark on her dress. He watched her like a hawk.

She looked up. She began to laugh. She laughed until tears ran down her cheeks.

"Oh, Don," she choked, between gales of laughter, "just because there is a groove in my dress, you think somebody took a shot at me. You're wonderful! All that build-up so you could propose to me in a new way. This is marvelous! You are so ingenuous in thinking up new ways to propose to me that I have half a mind to accept you."

Thunderstruck, the reporter stared at her. Was she stalling? Was she acting? "How did that hole get in your dress?" he demanded.

"I don't know," she confessed.

"You don't know?" he gasped.

"No. But I think I know. After I dressed this morning, I remembered there was a dress in the back of my closet that I wanted to leave out for the cleaner. I poked around in the closet after it and I must have caught myself on a nail. At least..." She bubbled over with laughter. "...at least I remember my collar catching on something, but I didn't think about it again—until now. Oh, Don, this is wonderful!"

Reed stared uneasily at her. The explanation she had given him sounded plausible. Suppose she was telling the truth? She *might* be. If she could really vanish when she wanted to, she was obviously something other than the girl she pretended to be and she would not be likely to admit to so strange an accomplishment. In that case, her denial proved nothing and her explanation of the origin of the hole in her dress collar proved only that she was quick-witted, which he already knew.

The reporter tried to continue his questioning. He was answered with gales of laughter.

"All right," he said at last. "Maybe I'm wrong. Maybe I'm crazy. If it wasn't for this..." He picked up the empty cartridge case. "...I would be willing to admit I'm crazy.

But this proves I saw a girl in a yellow dress almost get killed, and—"

The door suddenly burst open and a copy boy hastily entered the room.

"What do you want?" asked Don.

The lad flung a sheet of yellow paper on the desk in front of Nita Ayer.

"Big human interest story," he said. "Just came in over the wire. All about a naked man who was found in a plowed field. A lot of dead chickens mixed up in it somewhere. The boss says for Miss Ayer to get right on it and work it up."

The boy dashed out of the room again.

"A naked man found in a plowed field?" Reed gasped. "What the devil is this anyhow? Here, let me see that story..." He reached across the desk for the sheet of yellow paper.

Nita Ayer was already reading the story. All the color was going swiftly out of her cheeks as she read. Her eyes were widening with horror and growing fear.

"Oh, Don!" she gasped, looking up. "Oh, Don! It's happened!"

Pushing the sheet of paper ahead of her, she slumped down on the top of the desk in a faint.

## CHAPTER TWO
### *The Man from Nowhere*

DON REED spent a frantic few minutes determining that Nita had only fainted. He dashed to the water cooler, got a cup of water, and spilled most of it trying to get her to take a drink. Fortunately more competent hands than his appeared on the scene, hands that knew what to do when a girl fainted and Nita Ayer was promptly restored to consciousness.

She was much annoyed with herself for having fainted.

"Are you all right?" Reed asked anxiously.

"Of course, Don," she answered smiling at him. "There is really no need for you to look at me so frantically. A girl has a right to faint now and then."

"Not over this, she doesn't," Reed answered. He jerked his thumb toward the news story, which he had been hastily reading...

## FARMER FINDS NUDE MAN IN FIELD

John McCloy, who lives on a farm about two miles north of here, found an unclothed youth asleep in a plowed field yesterday morning. When awakened, the youth, who appears to be about nineteen years old, spoke in a strange language that no one in this vicinity understands. He was unable to give an account of himself, to tell where he had come from, or to tell why he had been sleeping in the field. He seemed totally unfamiliar with the most common objects of the farm and he appeared to be greatly frightened by the livestock. The sheriff, who was called to the scene by McCloy, removed the youth to the county jail, though no charges have been brought against him. The sheriff admits that he is baffled by the many unusual features of the case.

McCloy also reported that the same morning he found about half of his flock of chickens dead. The birds had been stabbed through the heart by some needle-like instrument. McCloy was unable to advance any reason for the destruction of the chickens or to suggest the means used in killing them.

The story had been filed from a small town in Wisconsin.

"Oh, that," Nita Ayer shrugged. "I didn't faint because of that."

"No?" said Reed.

"Of course not. Don," she said appealingly, "are you going to start asking those funny questions all over again?"

"Are you going up to Wisconsin to cover this story?" the reporter asked.

"Certainly," she said decisively. "Didn't you hear what the copy boy said?"

"Okay," the reporter answered. "I'm going with you."

"Don!" she quickly protested. "Really now. I'm the one who's being sent on the story, not you."

"That's all I wanted to know," Don Reed answered firmly. "Whether you like it or not, I'm going with you."

She didn't like it, she didn't like it even a little. She did everything she gracefully could do in order to keep him from accompanying her. He was adamant.

"But why do you want to go, Don?" she questioned. "After all, it's not so big a story that I can't handle it alone. Why do you want to go with me?"

"Shall we say it's because I enjoy your company?" He grinned at her. The grin was all on the surface. Inside he was as cold as ice. Before he left he went to his own desk and got the .32 caliber automatic pistol that he kept there. The gun had been bought for him by the *Globe*, as a result of a series of articles he had once written revealing intimate details of the life of a certain gangster, now deceased. The management of the *Globe*, taking heed of the threats the gangster was uttering, had thought he might need the gun to protect himself. He had never carried it, until today. He carefully inspected the mechanism to make certain it was in proper working order, filled the slide magazine with cartridges, and slipped the pistol in his pocket. Then he entered the lair of the managing editor and bluntly announced that he was accompanying Nita Ayer. There was an argument, the editor loudly shouting that he had a newspaper to get out and how in the hell was he going to do it if two of his best reporters went chasing off on a feature story?

"Fill it up with boiler plate!" the reporter said. "I'm going with Nita." That was that. A newspaper does not fire a star newsman for being an individual.

THEY made the trip in Reed's car. Nita, riding beside him, was thoughtful and silent.

"Don," she said at last. "What was back of those wild questions you were asking me?"

"That's what I'm trying to find out," he answered.

"Do you really think I was the girl you saw vanish?"

"What do you think?" he asked.

"Oh, don't be so evasive!"

Reed did not answer. He kept his eyes on the road. The girl seemed lost in thought.

"Don't you think," she said at last, "if somebody tried to kill me and I vanished, that I might not be a rather dangerous person?"

There was an impish glint in her eyes as she asked the question.

For some reason Reed felt the hairs rise on the back of his neck. Was she threatening him? If she could vanish at will, she certainly had strange powers.

He shook his head. "You're too beautiful to be dangerous," he said.

If she was teasing him, it was a game that two could play. If she would not answer the questions he asked, he would not answer the questions she asked. He was not absolutely positive she was the girl he had seen vanish, but he had grim suspicions.

They arrived in Rothmere, the town in which the story had originated, and found it a sleepy little country town, with few interests beyond the price of eggs, cheese, and crops. Reed wanted to go immediately to the jail and interview the strange youth who was being held there. Nita demurred.

"First, let's go talk to this farmer, McCloy, and see what he knows."

Reed agreed. It was as good a place to start as any.

McCloy lived in a small white house surrounded by neat, well-kept farm buildings. Behind the house was a plowed field of about ten acres.

There were a million farm homes that looked like this in the United States, Reed thought as he went up to knock on the door of the house. Some of them maybe looked more prosperous than this one; some of them didn't. The door opened to his knock. A gray-haired stoop-shouldered man with large gnarled hands and wrinkled, leathery cheeks stood there.

"Mr. McCloy?" Reed said. He introduced himself, then introduced Nita.

"You reporters?" McCloy asked. "Come in. Come in." He seemed flattered to think that a newspaper would send reporters all the way from Chicago to talk to him. He led them into a small sitting room and introduced them to a motherly woman who was Mrs. McCloy.

"Sit down and make yourself at home," McCloy said. He seated himself in a cane-bottomed rocking chair.

Leaning against the wall within easy reach of his hand was a repeating shotgun. "What can I do for you?"

"We're doing a story about the nude youth you found the other morning," Reed answered. "We would like to hear what you can tell us about him."

"Oh," McCloy said, in a low tone of voice. He looked questioningly at his wife. "You want to know about him." He sat in thoughtful silence for a moment. He glanced at Nita Ayer and then quickly away, his gaze coming back to the girl again and again. Something about her seemed to fascinate him.

"How did you find him?" Reed prompted.

McCloy looked at his wife to see if she thought he ought to answer this question. She nodded with perceptible hesitancy.

"I was going out to the barn," the farmer said. "It was maybe a quarter of four in the morning; sun wasn't up yet. First thing I noticed was that the cattle were all huddled up in a corner of the barn lot like they were scared."

"Had you heard anything during the night?" Reed questioned.

"Nope. Except that the dog barked a lot along toward morning. I didn't pay any attention to him, thought maybe a goat had got out of the pen and he was barkin' at it."

"What about this young man?" Reed asked.

"He was right out in the middle of the plowed field back of the house," McCloy answered uneasily. "I walked out to him. First, I thought he was dead, but then I touched him, and he woke up."

"What did he say?" Reed questioned.

"I don't know what he said. He spoke all right but I couldn't understand what he was saying."

"What did you do with him?"

"I brought him in the house. We hunted up some clothes for him and my wife fixed up some breakfast in the kitchen for him."

The farmer's voice went into silence. "I can't even begin to understand that young man," Mrs. McCloy spoke. She looked at Reed. "He didn't even know how to eat."

"What do you mean?" the reporter questioned.

"I fixed him up a nice breakfast of ham and scrambled eggs. He ate them with his fingers."

"With his fingers?" the reporter asked, a little surprised.

"He acted like he didn't know how to use a knife and fork," Mrs. McCloy said firmly. "I honestly believe he had never seen a knife and fork before in all his life."

Reed started to protest that this was impossible but caught the words before they were uttered. How did he know what was possible and what wasn't?

"Was there anything else about him?" he asked.

The farmer hesitated. He had something else on his mind but he didn't much want too talk about it. The reporter prodded him.

"There's one thing I can't understand at all," he said at last.

"What is that?" Reed questioned.

"I found him in the middle of a plowed field," McCloy answered slowly. "The ground was soft. After I had brought him in the house I went back to the field and followed his tracks to see where he had come from. His footprints were plain enough. The danged thing is, they went along for thirty or forty yards *and then they disappeared!*"

HE LOOKED at the reporter as if he expected this statement to be challenged. Reed realized that a part of

McCloy's hesitancy was due to the fact that he had told this story before and it *had* been challenged. Men had been laughing at McCloy's story and he had become sensitive about telling it.

There was silence in the room. Outside the house a watchdog barked.

At the sound, McCloy reached quickly for the shotgun leaning against the wall, picked it up, and stepped to the window.

Not until then did the reporter fully realize how badly scared this farmer was. He looked at Nita Ayer. She was biting her lips and her face was set in an emotionless mask. Skin crawled along Reed's back.

"What is it?" he asked.

McCloy didn't answer. He stared out of the window, the gun held ready. Reed could hear the big clock on the shelf ticking sluggishly. Somewhere in the distance a cow bawled. McCloy leaned the gun against the wall and sat back down.

"It wasn't anything," he said. "Old Shep has been barking the last couple of days like now and then he sees something he don't like."

"Have you seen anything?" Reed asked.

The farmer shook his head.

"What do you think the dog sees?" the reporter persisted.

"Golly, mister, I don't know," McCloy answered.

"How do you think this young man you found got in the middle of your field?" Reed asked, changing the subject.

"I don't know how to answer that either," the farmer answered. "But if you want to come and take a look for yourself, I'll show you where I found him and you can try to figure out for yourself how he got there."

Reed rose with alacrity. "Coming?" he said to Nita.

"I—I—I don't believe so," the girl faltered. "I think I'll stay here and talk to Mrs. McCloy."

Her face was tense and colorless. Reed looked keenly at her. "Are you scared about something?" he demanded.

"N—no," Nita said quickly. "I just thought I would stay here and talk to Mrs. McCloy so I could get her angle for the story."

"All right," Reed said. He followed the farmer out of the house. McCloy, with a glance at his wife, left the shotgun behind, and Reed, in a flash of intuition, wondered if he was leaving the gun for her to use if she needed it. "Holy cats…" he wondered. "What's going on here?"

In the backyard a shaggy-coated shepherd watchdog joined them. The dog ran quickly to McCloy. When they went into the field back of the house it followed them with reluctance.

"I found him right here," the farmer said, pointing to a spot in the middle of the field. "His tracks went back to right there." He pointed to another spot about thirty-five yards away.

"Holy hell…" Reed gasped. "Did he drop from the sky or something?"

There was no other obvious solution. The youth had appeared in the middle of a plowed field. The soft soil would certainly retain his footprints. But his footprints did not go near the edge of the field.

"That's what some of these wise guys around here said when I tried to tell them the truth," McCloy answered sullenly. "You don't have to believe me if you don't want to. I'm telling you what I saw and what I found. You can take it or leave it."

"No offense," Reed said, quickly apologizing. "But can you suggest any explanation for the way his tracks disappeared?"

"I can't suggest anything," McCloy answered. "My wife and I have been worrying ourselves sick about it. No matter how you twist it or turn it, it don't make sense. At first I thought maybe he had dropped from an airplane, but he would have needed a parachute to do that, and no parachute has been found. All I can say is that he must have *landed* in the field, ran a few feet, then collapsed, but mister, if you ask me where he came from, I sure can't tell you."

REED did not doubt that McCloy was telling the truth. There was an air of dogged honesty about the farmer that was completely convincing. Farmers usually weren't liars. But where had the mysterious youth come from? What was he doing here? Why had Nita Ayer been so frightened when she first read about him?

Cold chills were playing all over Reed's body.

"He was completely naked?" he asked.

"Well, almost," McCloy answered hesitantly.

"Then he did have on some clothing?" the reporter questioned.

"You couldn't exactly call it clothing," the farmer said. He looked keenly at Reed. "Mister," he said suddenly, "What do you know about that girl who came here with you?"

"Why, everything, nothing," Reed said dumfoundedly. "She works with me. What's she got to do with this?"

"I don't know that she's got anything to do with this," McCloy answered. "But I do know she's wearing a damned funny bracelet and I know this young man I found was wearing the same kind of a bracelet. It was the only thing he had on in the way of clothing, a bracelet. That's one reason I haven't been too anxious to talk to you, mister, because that bracelet had the same kind of big gray jewel in it that the girl who came with you is wearing!"

Reed rocked back on his heels. The information stunned him. He remembered perfectly the bracelet Nita wore. Never, since he had known her, had he seen her without it.

"But—" he gasped. The sudden sharp bark of the watchdog interrupted him. He turned quickly around. The dog was running across the field away from them. As it ran it was snapping back over its shoulder as if it was trying to bite something that was closely pursuing it. Its tail was tucked between its legs and it was running as hard as it could.

Suddenly it yelped in pain. Its muscles suddenly seemed to be without strength. It floundered along the ground, twisted, turned a somersault, tried to crawl along. It howled, its muzzle lifted to the sky. The howl died into sudden silence.

By the time Reed and McCloy reached it, the dog was dead. A tiny spot of blood marred its coat. Reed spread the fur aside. There was a small pinprick in the dog's side.

"Stabbed through the heart!" McCloy gasped. "Something stabbed it through the heart, just like something killed my chickens!"

The farmer's eyes were roving over the plowed field. He seemed to be looking for something and not seeing it.

Reed made a hasty survey of the scene. If there was anything in the field, he couldn't see it.

And yet the dog had acted as if it had been chased by some invisible being, something that it could see or smell, but which a human could not see!

Reed looked everywhere. Nothing moved in the plowed field. McCloy, standing beside him, was also looking. They saw nothing. At their feet the dog lay dead.

## CHAPTER THREE
### *Merthu*

REED drove the car back to Rothmere. Beside him, Nita Ayer was pale and silent. He had not as yet mentioned the death of the dog. When they had returned from the field, McCloy had not said anything about it either, but as soon as he entered the house, the farmer had picked up the gun.

On the girl's left wrist, Reed could see the bracelet. It was set with a single large jewel that looked like a moonstone. Curved to shape the wrist, the bracelet was made of a single piece of some metal that looked like bronze. It was engraved with incredibly, delicate figures and Reed had the momentary impression that these figures might be some strange form of writing, but what the language was—if it was a language—he could not begin to guess. It looked a little like Hebrew script and it also seemed to resemble the cuneiform of the Babylonians as well as the hieroglyphics of the ancient Egyptians—three languages blended into one. He decided it was pure ornamentation.

"What did you find in the field?" Nita asked.

"A dead dog," Reed answered.

"A *what?*" she gasped.

He told her how the dog had died.

As she listened she seemed to shrink into herself. Her face was calm and composed and no trace of tension showed on it but twice he noticed that she glanced furtively over her shoulder and out of the rear window of the car.

"That's odd," she said when he had finished. "What do you think killed the dog?"

"I don't know," he said. "I thought perhaps you might be able to offer a suggestion."

She looked startled. "I haven't the slightest idea," she said quickly, glancing at him. "What made you think I did?"

Reed shrugged. In his work he had interviewed many a person who was reluctant to talk but he had never found one who was so clever at evading questions as Nita Ayer.

Or was he misjudging her? Was she entirely innocent? When he thought she knew more than she was telling, was he completely mistaken?

He did not know. But he did sense that he was on the trail of a terrible mystery; he suspected it was so terrible that the people who knew anything about it were most reluctant to talk. He had seen a girl vanish, he had seen a man vanish, he had seen a dog run from something that he could not see, and he had seen the dog die. He pressed his arm against his pocket. There was little comfort in the feel of the pistol nestled there. What good would a gun have been against the thing that had killed the dog?

WHEN they arrived in Rothmere, Reed said, "Well, the next thing on the schedule is to hunt up the jail and interview the fellow who was found in the field."

"Why don't you interview him?" Nita said.

"You mean by myself?"

"Yes," Nita said quickly. "While you're seeing him, I'll talk to the people around town and get their angle on the story."

"Don't you want to see him?" the reporter questioned. "He's the most important part of this business."

"There's no need for both of us seeing him," she suggested.

Reed hesitantly agreed. The suggestion she had made was in line with accepted newspaper practice. When two reporters are assigned to the same story, each covers a different angle, but Reed had the suspicion that Nita, for some reason she was not revealing, did not want to interview the strange youth. There was nothing he could do about it however. Dropping Nita in front of the only hotel the town afforded, they made a date to meet there in an hour, and Reed went on to the jail.

Reed did not know what he was expecting to find at the jail, but ever since he had heard McCloy's story, he had been extremely curious about the youth who had miraculously appeared in the farmer's field.

The sheriff was a tall, raw-boned individual named Clanning. "Another reporter?" he said, when Reed had produced his credentials. "Sure, you can see him."

"Are there other reporters on the story already?" Reed asked.

"Three others here right now," the sheriff answered. He held up his hand for silence, jerked a thumb toward a closed door, and grinned. "Listen," he said.

From the room adjoining the sheriff's office came the sound of angry voices. One voice, an angry, bull-bellow, was raised above all the rest.

"Idiots!" the voice was shouting. "Stupidities! It is no sense that reporters have at all!"

THERE was a moment of silence, then another, quieter voice said, "It isn't that we don't have any sense, Professor. We run into so many fakers that we don't believe anybody. Now in your case, we certainly aren't saying we don't believe you. All we are asking you to do is produce the goods. You claim to know where Merthu came from. All right. Prove it."

An angry growl came from beyond the door.

"Who's in there?" Reed asked curiously.

The sheriff chuckled. "The reporters are in there. They are interviewing Professor Harker."

"It sounds like they're giving him the needle," Reed said, grinning. "Who is he?"

"I do not know," the sheriff answered. "He is some blow-hard who turned up here this morning and said he knew where Merthu came from."

"Ah. And who is Merthu?"

"I forgot you didn't know. He's the boy that McCloy found in his field."

"I see," Reed said. "How did you learn his name? I thought he could not speak any known language."

"Nor can he. He points to himself and says 'Merthu.' That's why we think his name is Merthu. But come with me. I'll take you to his cell."

"Incidentally," Reed said, as he followed the sheriff back into the small jail. "Why have you kept him locked up?"

"I haven't kept him locked up," the sheriff replied. "He is keeping himself locked up, by refusing to come out of his cell."

"He won't come out?" the reporter asked ponderingly. "That's odd. Why won't he?"

"I don't know that either," the sheriff said, shaking his head. "I think he's afraid to come out. Ah. Here he is. You can see for yourself."

The sheriff unlocked the door and Reed entered the small cell. Crouched like some frightened animal on the lower bunk of the double-decker bed was Merthu. Apparently someone had given him clothing for he was wearing a khaki shirt and a pair of wrinkled trousers. He didn't move a muscle when the reporter entered the cell but his eyes were fixed on Reed's face with unwavering intensity. Again the reporter had the impression that Merthu looked like an animal that, suspecting the presence of the hunter, is too frightened to move and can only crouch and wait for the death it fears is coming.

Reed smiled. It was an easy smile, the kind that invites confidence. "Hello," he said.

Merthu did not move. His eyes were fixed on Reed's face in a look in which fear and pathetic longing were mingled.

"You don't need to be afraid of me," Reed said. "I'm not going to hurt you."

He had no hope that the youth would understand the words but the tone in which they were spoken might carry meaning. It seemed to work. A little of the fear went out of Merthu's eyes.

"*Se?*" he said. "*Du quetchen se?*" His voice was soft and liquid.

"Sorry, I can't understand you, old man," Reed said. "And what I would give to be able to understand you…"

If he could only understand the language spoken by this frightened youth! The catch was, he couldn't. Apparently no one in this vicinity could understand the language. All secrets that Merthu might possess were locked in his own mind.

Reed did not doubt that Merthu did possess secrets. Outwardly he looked much like an ordinary human boy about nineteen or twenty years old. A dozen characteristics betrayed the difference. The color of his skin was a golden tan, almost a bronze, his features were finer, more delicately molded, than those of the average human, and there was a *strangeness* about him, an eerie weirdness that would not go into words, that was quite unlike the average man.

And yet Merthu had to be human. What else could he be?

UNABLE to talk to Merthu, Reed was forced to get all his information about the youth by just looking at him. There was one thing in particular that he wanted to see—the bracelet. It was easily visible. By signs the reporter indicated that he wanted to look at it and Merthu reluctantly extended his arm.

A glance was enough to tell Reed what he wanted to know. *The bracelet was exactly the same as the ornament Nita wore.* There was only one difference: the stone in Merthu's bracelet was broken. It was still held within its clasp but it was broken into two pieces. Somehow the fact that it was broken seemed to cause it to lose some of its life. The moonstone in Nita's bracelet had a peculiar shimmer almost as if it glowed with hidden, inner fires, but the stone in this bracelet was dull and lifeless.

"Where did you get that bracelet?" Reed demanded. "Who are you, anyhow? Where did you come from? Oh, damn it, why can't you talk?"

Merthu, startled by the tone, drew back into the corner. Putting the bracelet arm behind him, he stared at the reporter in doubtful fear.

"Sorry, old man," Reed apologized. "I didn't mean to snap at you. But damn it, I would give a fortune if you could only speak a language I could understand."

There was a link between Merthu and Nita Ayer! The bracelet proved it. But Nita, for reasons of her own, wouldn't talk, and Merthu couldn't. Reed had the solution to the mystery right before his eyes and couldn't solve it. If only Merthu could talk!

"Damn it, I'm going to get every language expert in the country down here!" the reporter exploded. "Somebody knows your language. Somebody can understand you. I'm going to find out what is back of you or die trying."

"No need is there for that," a voice boomed from outside the cell. "I can understand the language spoken by this young man. I, the great Harker, will be glad to interpret for you…"

Startled, Reed looked up. The door of the cell was thrust open. A short, thickset and apparently exceedingly strong man stood in the door. He was dressed neatly in a black suit and he had a square, flat face adorned by a pointed beard. From behind thick-lensed spectacles, black eyes snapped at everything within their range of vision.

"Who the devil are you?" Reed demanded.

The question seemed to astound the man. "You do not know of the great Harker?" he demanded. "Permit me to introduce myself." Bowing from the waist, he extended a card to the reporter.

Engraved on the card were the words:

## JAMES RANDOLPH HARKER
*Messenger from the hidden world.*

"Oh," Reed said, struggling to repress a grin. "You're the fellow I heard talking to the reporters?"

"That I am." Harker said. "Anyhow I was talking to them. I can only take your statement that you overheard me. Hah! Such damned fools as those reporters are I never thought existed in this world. Trying to explain the great truths to them was casting pearls before swine." He glared suspiciously at Reed. "You are not a reporter, are you?"

"Well, yes," Reed admitted.

"And are you also a fool?" Harker asked.

"At times I feel like one," Reed answered. "But if you can talk to Merthu—"

"Of course I can talk to him." Harker interrupted, glaring at the reporter. "What do you want to ask him?"

"Ask him where he came from."

"I don't need to ask him that," Harker said bluntly. "I already know where he came from—*the hidden world.*"

REED rocked back on his heels. The calm assurance of this man was bewildering and annoying. No wonder the reporters had given him the needle. Newsmen loved nothing better than to catch a quack.

"Where is the hidden world?" Reed questioned.

Harker smiled blandly. "That is a secret reserved for those initiates who have completed their instructions," he stated pompously. "Such secrets are never imparted to common men. Now," he turned to Merthu, "since you desire it, I will demonstrate my ability to converse with this ah—runaway."

Reed choked off a desire to be sarcastic. After all, suppose this fellow could talk to Merthu!

Harker spoke a string of syllables that Reed did not understand. He looked at Merthu to see if the youth gave any evidence that he understood them.

Merthu had drawn as far away as he could get. He was still sitting on the lower deck of the bed. He had drawn himself into as tight a knot as possible and was back in the corner against the wall. He did not answer.

Harker spoke again.

Merthu gave no indication that he had even heard the words.

Reed lit a cigarette. He looked at Harker and grinned.

The grin drove Harker into a fury. "He understands me," he said, raising his voice. "He just refuses to talk. He knows every word I have spoken."

"That's too bad," Reed said, in mock sympathy. "Now if you'll excuse me, I think I have seen enough." Still grinning, he left the cell. Harker glared furiously at him as he left.


REED drove back to the hotel to meet Nita. She wasn't at the hotel. He sat down to wait for her. An hour passed. Nita did not come.

Sheriff Clanning entered the lobby. He looked around, saw Reed, and came straight toward him.

"You're under arrest," the sheriff said.

"I—what?" the reporter gasped.

"You're under arrest," the sheriff repeated. "Get your hands up and don't try anything."

The dazed reporter found himself looking into the muzzle of a gun. He lifted his hands. Steel cuffs clicked on his wrists.

"You can't arrest me like this," he protested. "What are you charging me with? I haven't committed any crime."

"I am arresting you," the sheriff said grimly. "If you want to know the charge, it's accessory before the fact."

Reed stared in stupefied amazement at the officer. "Accessory before *what* fact?" he demanded. "Have you gone crazy?"

The sheriff studied him. "I'm willing to admit that you may be innocent," he said. "But I'm not taking any chances. If you're innocent, you will have a chance to prove it. If you are interested in the charge, it's murder!"

Reed did not believe his ears. He was being charged with murder. It was impossible. It was mad!

"That's insane!" he blurted. "I haven't killed anybody. I can account for every minute of my time."

"I said the charge was murder," the sheriff answered. "I didn't say you had committed the murder. I said you were charged with being an accessory before the fact—"

"That means I helped somebody commit murder," Reed protested. "That's ridiculous and I can prove it. Who was killed?"

"Merthu," the sheriff answered.

"Merthu!" Reed gasped. "But he was all right when I left him. Who—" His eyes dug into the sheriff's face. "Who did kill him?"

His thought was that Harker had killed the bronze youth and had succeeded in convincing the sheriff that Reed had helped him. Harker would have an obvious motive for bringing such a charge. Reed, as a reporter, would have a wealthy and powerful newspaper to help defend him. If the reporter were jointly charged with the crime, Harker would automatically get first-class legal assistance, free.

"Harker was in my presence when the crime was committed," the sheriff said. "He didn't kill Merthu. Merthu was killed by the young woman you brought down here with you, he was killed by *Nita Ayer!*"

Reed was too dumbfounded to attempt to protest as the sheriff led him away. Two thoughts were burning in his mind.

Merthu was dead.

Nita Ayer was charged with his murder.

## CHAPTER FOUR
*Nita's Story*

"HOW was Merthu killed?" Reed hotly demanded. They were in the sheriff's office at the jail. Reed had been searched and the pistol had been found on him. It did him little good to protest that he had a permit to carry the pistol in Chicago. Such a permit was no good in Wisconsin. The sheriff and two grim-faced deputies were present.

"He was stabbed through the heart with a long needle," the sheriff answered.

"With a needle—" He stopped, appalled. He had seen a dog die suddenly from a stab through the heart. McCloy had said his chickens had died the same way. Now Merthu—

"How do you know that Nita Ayer killed him?" Reed demanded. "Did you see her do it?"

"No," the sheriff reluctantly said.

"She came to the jail as soon as you left. It is my personal opinion..." He looked meaningly at Reed. "...that she waited until you were gone before she came here. At least one of my men..." He nodded toward one of the deputies. "...noticed her waiting around the corner.

She seemed to be watching the entrance of the jail and as soon as you left, she came hurrying in and wanted to talk to Merthu. I granted her request. I had no choice except to grant it. Almost as soon as she entered his cell, we heard a scream. We went to him. We found Merthu dying and this girl was trying to escape."

In the face of such damning evidence, there was little that Reed could do. And—worst of all—Nita had tricked *him.* He knew now why she had suggested that he see Merthu while she talked to the townspeople. She wanted to get away from him so she could see Merthu alone. She entered the jail as soon as he had left; she had been seen waiting around the corner.

One conclusion was obvious. There was some connection between Nita and Merthu. Equally obvious was the fact that she knew a lot more than she was telling.

"I want to talk to her," Reed said.

Getting his request granted took some doing, including a long distance call to Chicago and a hot exchange of words between the sheriff and the *Globe's* managing editor. The sheriff reluctantly agreed. Reed was taken to her cell.

A second after he entered, she was in his arms. "I didn't do it, Don," she was sobbing. "I didn't. I *didn't!* You've got to believe me, Don. I didn't kill him."

"Who did kill him?" Reed said.

"The *hurthen* killed him," Nita Ayer sobbed. "It followed us from the farm. I was afraid it was following us, and when we got here I tried to throw it off the trail. But somehow it managed to follow us. Don, I didn't kill him, I swear I didn't. The *hurthen* killed him."

"The *what?*" Reed gasped.

"The *hurthen,*" Nita Ayer said. "You can't see it. The only way you can tell it's near is by feeling something like a cold wind blowing on you. The *hurthen* is invisible. But it's cold, like a snake. You can feel the coldness of it. That is the only way you can tell a *hurthen* is near—"

She broke off, stared at him with suddenly frightened eyes.

"What are you saying?" Reed whispered. *"A hurthen— cold winds*—Nita, what are you talking about?"

*"Don! Don! Don!"* Terror was alive in her eyes. "Forget I ever said that! Don, you *must* forget what I said! You must not believe me! Don, I am out of my head. I am insane!" Sobbing she threw herself on the lower deck of the bed and buried her head in the pillow.

REED sat down on the edge of the bed. Gently he took her hands in his. "I'm your friend, Nita," he said.

"Go away," she sobbed.

"I'm not going away," he said. "I'm staying right here until you tell me what this is all about."

"I can't tell you," she whispered. "I didn't kill Merthu."

"I know you didn't," he said gently. "Why did you go to him?"

"I wanted to talk to him. I wanted to find out why he was here. Even if the *hurthen* was following me, I did not think Merthu would be in danger. I thought he had protection. Tell me, Don!" she sat up and looked frantically at Reed. "Did you see Merthu before I did?"

"Yes," the reporter said.

"Did you notice whether or not he was wearing a bracelet—like the one I wear?"

"He was," Reed said. "I saw it."

"Was—was—" Again there was terror in her eyes. "Was the bracelet all right? I mean—was it broken, or damaged, or anything?"

"The stone was cracked," Reed answered. "What does that mean, Nita? I paid particular attention to the bracelet and the stone was broken. Was that important?"

"Oh, yes!" the girl gasped. "If the stone had not been broken, the *hurthen* would not have been able to touch him. I've been going frantic wondering about that. I was afraid Merthu's death meant they had discovered a way to overcome the power of the bracelet. I knew he was wearing a bracelet, but I did not know whether or not it was broken. Oh, Don, I'm glad you told me this."

Relief flooded through her voice. She had been on the verge of panic. But her words brought no relief to Don Reed.

"Nita," he demanded. "Will you please tell me what this is all about?"

Panic came back to her face as he spoke. She seemed to realize what she had been saying.

"Oh, Don, I didn't mean to tell you that!" she gasped.

"But I've got a right to know," he insisted. "Remember, I'm mixed up in this business too. What is a *hurthen?* Where did Merthu come from? Where did *you* come from? Where did you get your bracelet? What is the bracelet? Nita, you've got to talk."

"I won't talk," she wailed. "I can't."

"You've got to," Reed doggedly insisted.

"Don, I don't dare," she answered.

"But you must, Nita. Why don't you?"

Tears glistened in her eyes. "I didn't mean to tell you this, Don. I meant to go away, so you would never know. You would forget me, if I went away—"

"What are you talking about?" he interrupted.

The tears were rolling down her cheeks now.

"I love you, Don. That's what I'm talking about."

111

"You—" The suddenness of the admission left Reed speechless. It seemed to him that ever since he had first met this girl he had been in love with her, but until now he had had no inkling that she also loved him. His heart skipped a beat, then raced. "Nita—" he whispered.

"I love you, Don," she repeated. She dabbled at the tears with a tiny crumpled handkerchief. "That's why I won't tell you who I am or what I am."

"But Nita!" he insisted. "That is all the more reason why you should tell me."

"No, it isn't," she repeated. "It's a perfect reason why I should not tell you."

"Why?" he demanded.

"Because the knowledge I have means death!" The words were forced from her lips. "If I tell you what I know, they will kill you, Don, just as they killed Merthu, to make certain he would never talk, just as they will kill me, if they can, just as they have tried to kill me so many times, and failed. D—Don, do you understand now why I won't talk?"

DAZEDLY Don Reed stared at her. She had given him a convincing reason for her silence. She loved him. She didn't want him to die. If she told him what she knew, he would be killed. That was what she thought.

"That may be," Reed said grimly. "But I'll take some killing, Nita. I've had a few hot shots after me before now and I'm still alive and kicking."

"You wouldn't have a chance against the Dark Ones, Don. No more chance than Merthu had, when the *hurthen* came and found him defenseless. Nor do they have to kill by sending a *hurthen* to stab their victims through the heart. They would be near you and you would never know it.

Maybe all that would happen would be that your heart would suddenly stop beating. There would be no wound, no sign to indicate the cause of death. Anyone, even the best doctor in the country, would think you had died of heart failure. You would know what had killed you, but you would never be able to reveal your knowledge. You would die too quickly. Believe me, Don, I know what I am talking about. For your safety, I dare not talk."

She talked earnestly, in a soft, tense voice. Night was coming and shadows were creeping into the cell. The light had not been turned on.

"Do you think I'm a sissy, Nita?" Reed argued. "I'm not afraid."

"I know you aren't afraid," she answered. "That is another reason why I won't tell you what I know. If you were afraid, you might have a chance."

"Who are the Dark Ones?" Reed said doggedly.

But Nita had regained complete control of herself. She had spoken only under the compulsion of panic and fear. Now she had her emotions under control. She refused to answer another question.

"No, Don," was all she would say, accompanied by a firm shake of the head.

"But what are we going to do?" he protested. "Remember, you are charged with murder. Merthu was killed when you were with him. You will never be able to convince a jury that he was stabbed by some invisible creature that you call a *hurthen*. I hate to say it, Nita, but you're in a tough spot, and you are going to need all the help you can get."

"Don't worry about that," she answered. "I will never face a jury."

"But you won't have any choice, unless..." He hesitated, then blurted out the words, "...unless you are going to plead insanity, in which case the verdict will be an insane asylum. Nita, you've got to talk. You've got to tell me everything, so I can try to help you."

His protests were useless.

"TIME'S up," a voice spoke from outside of the cell. A deputy entered. Reed was taken to the office of the sheriff.

"Sit down, Reed," Sheriff Clanning said.

"Well?" Reed said, slumping into a chair. He was aware that the sheriff was staring fixedly at him.

"That was a strange story the young lady told you," the sheriff spoke at last.

"You listened?"

"Naturally," the sheriff nodded. "I had my secretary in the next cell taking notes in shorthand. What do you make of her story, Reed?"

"I'm damned if I know," the reporter blurted out. "She didn't kill Merthu. I'm convinced of that. There was some connection between them but I don't know what it was. I don't know who she really is or where she came from or anything about her, actually. But I do know that she is up against the toughest proposition that any human being ever faced."

"Yes," the sheriff gravely agreed. "Murder is a serious matter. Even if you are innocent, a murder charge is a serious thing."

"Hell, I'm not thinking about that murder charge," Reed snapped. "I'm thinking about the Dark Ones, whatever they are. That's what she is up against—the Dark Ones."

Unbidden into his mind came the mental picture of dark creatures moving furtively on earth. The thought was sinister. A cold wind suddenly seemed to blow on him. He leaped to his feet, looked wildly around the office.

"What is it?" the sheriff s aid, alarmed.

"I thought—I thought something cold touched me," Reed whispered. "But it was nothing."

Except for the normal furnishing of the place, the office was empty but Reed had the haunting feeling that he was being watched, that somewhere sinister forces were coldly calculating how much he knew.

He forced himself to sit back down. If there was a *hurthen* in the office, there was nothing he could do. The *hurthen*, Nita had said, was invisible. The only way you knew it was near you was by a feeling of cold…

As Reed sat down, the door of the office opened. A startled deputy entered. "Hey, sheriff!" he shouted. "She's gone!"

"What?" Clanning demanded. "What are you talking about? Who is gone?"

"The girl we're holding on a murder charge," the deputy said. "Nita Ayer. I just looked in her cell and she wasn't there."

"Escaped? Are you crazy?" the sheriff demanded. "How could she have escaped?"

"I—I don't know," the deputy answered. "All I know is she's gone."

Clanning got energetically to his feet. He did not object when Reed followed him and the deputy back to the cell where Nita had been held prisoner.

The reporter watched the perturbed sheriff examine the door. It was still locked. The deputy produced a key and the three men entered. They made a thorough examination. The walls were of stone reinforced with steel.

The windows were heavily barred. The lock had not been tampered with.

Nita Ayer was gone.

The sheriff looked at Reed. "Did you have anything to do with this?" he demanded.

Reed shook his head. He did not trust himself to speak.

"You were the last person who was with her," the sheriff insisted.

"So what?" Reed questioned.

"Maybe you gave her a key to the lock," Clanning suggested. "Maybe as soon as you left, she opened the door, and slipped out the back way."

"Maybe I had a key to give her!" Reed snorted.

"I didn't think of that," Clanning said thoughtfully. "Well, we'll soon know how she escaped. She can't be far away. She hasn't had time to get far. I'll put in a call to block all roads. We'll pick her up all right."

"I'll give you odds of ten to one you don't pick her up," Reed said.

"What do you mean by that?" Clanning demanded. "Of course we'll catch her. This is a small town. There are only three main roads leading out of it. She won't have a chance to escape. In a big city she might be hard to find, but here it'll be easy."

Reed kept silent. Although he was technically still under arrest, he was allowed to return to the sheriff's office. There he listened while Clanning put out a general call for Nita Ayer.

An hour passed. Reed knew that all around the town of Rothmere the roads were blocked. Pick-up orders had gone out over the air. Within a fifty-mile radius all cars were being stopped and their occupants investigated.

Deputy sheriffs were scouring the town of Rothmere and the surrounding country.

They hadn't found Nita Ayer.

At midnight they were still searching. They weren't having any luck. The search was relentless and grim, but Nita Ayer couldn't have disappeared more effectively if she had walked off the face of the earth.

"Anyhow this proves she was guilty of killing Merthu," Clanning said. "If she wasn't guilty, why would she run away?"

It was a question Reed could not answer, even to his own satisfaction. Why had Nita run away? She had said she would never face a jury. Had she meant that she was going to escape? Also, how had she escaped? That was the confounding question. How had she escaped from a locked, barred cell?

## CHAPTER FIVE
### *The Search for Nita Ayer*

THREE days later, Nita Ayer was still missing.

Don Reed had been released on bond. The fact that he had been released at all showed that the office of the prosecuting attorney felt it had a very slim case against him. Or no case at all. Reed knew his full release was inevitable. The prosecution simply did not have enough evidence to convict Nita Ayer of murdering Merthu, and they had no case at all against him. He moved into the local hotel.

The hunt for Nita Ayer was dying down. Clanning had started the hunt with a great deal of determination. The more time the sheriff had to think about it, the less vigorously he prosecuted the search. The sheriff had reasons for letting the hunt die down, good reasons.

The first reason was the way Nita Ayer had escaped. There were two alternatives, one, that she had opened the lock with a key. But there were only two keys. The sheriff had one and his deputy who served as jailer had the other. Therefore, if she had used a key to escape, she had either bribed the sheriff or his deputy. Even if this had not happened, the sheriff knew if there was much talk around town about it, a lot of people would believe that he or his deputy had accepted a bribe. Clanning had been elected to his office. If the voters got the idea he could be bribed, he would not be re-elected.

The second way that Nita Ayer could have escaped involved the supernatural. No one in a public office and in his right mind would under any circumstances admit the existence of the supernatural, for the obvious reason that if such an admission did not get him impeached, it would certainly be used against him in the next election.

The sheriff was caught in something a little worse than a dilemma. As soon as he had time to think about the matter, he took the one course open to him—he shut up tighter than a clam. The office of the prosecuting attorney, which had first sensed a sensational murder mystery with its consequent publicity, shut up with him. The sheriff and the prosecuting attorney examined the facts and found them not at all to their liking.

The facts were:

A naked youth had appeared in a plowed field under mysterious circumstances, a youth who could not talk English or any other known language.

This youth had been murdered while he was securely held in jail.

The girl who had at first been charged with his murder had vanished from a locked, barred cell.

There was no natural, easy explanation for any of these facts. The only way to explain them was by the supernatural.

The fourth day after Nita Ayer had escaped, the sheriff issued a guarded explanation to the effect that "Nita Ayer was possibly not guilty of murder, as he had first thought." Then he got busy chasing a gang of tire thieves.

The prosecuting attorney issued a statement that, "While this case is not closed, until new evidence is brought to light, no further action can be taken." The prosecuting attorney then went on a fishing trip.

Both of them fervently hoped that the public would speedily forget the whole thing. They wanted to forget it too. Both of them secretly knew that a supernatural mystery had been dumped in their laps. They wanted no part of it.

DON REED, still staying in the local hotel, received with no enthusiasm the news that he was no longer charged with complicity in the murder of Merthu. He had seen the haste with which the case had been dropped and he clearly understood the actions of the sheriff and the prosecuting attorney. He had not written and had not attempted to write a single line of the real story for his own paper. A few other reporters, attracted by the sensational promise of the news, had come into town. After investigating the story, they had departed as swiftly as they came, without writing a word about it. Like the sheriff, they had good reasons for their actions:

If they wrote the stories, their papers would not publish them.

Newspapers have a reputation for veracity to maintain. If they published a story like this, their readers would either call them liars or laugh at the ingenuity of the reporters. Hence, no stories were written. The supernatural is sternly censored out of the newspapers or is buried among the opium dreams of the feature sections.

Don Reed, viewing the operation of this system of censorship which promptly clamped down to prevent the publication of news of a supernatural nature, was struck by a sudden thought: How many other supernatural events occur daily on earth and never get mentioned in the newspapers?

How many times have strangers been observed in fields, their presence reported only by farmers who doubt their own eyes? How many people have actually seen ghosts and been afraid to talk of their experience for fear of being ridiculed?

The thought had shuddery implications. It was possible that every day on earth people saw astounding things happen.

In this particular case, Don Reed had seen too much to have any doubt that he had come into first-hand contact with what could only be called supernatural. He had all the facts the sheriff had. In addition, he knew he had seen Nita Ayer vanish. The girl in the yellow dress had been Nita.

She had escaped from the jail in the same way she had escaped from the man who had tried to kill her.

Also, he knew what Nita had told him. She had told him precious little, he thought bitterly. She had talked of the Dark Ones and of a *hurthen* and had refused to tell him anything more in an effort to save his own life. She had said that knowledge was deadly. He knew, as he made the decision, that he was walking headlong into danger, but he also knew that he would never rest until he found Nita

Ayer. Where ever she had gone, he would find her. He would solve this mystery.

The first problem was to find Nita. She was the key that would unlock all doors. If she could be found and convinced she ought to talk, she could explain about the Dark Ones, about Merthu, about the *hurthen*.

How to find her?

Don Reed returned to Chicago, reported back to his newspaper office, prepared to resume the old routine of work. As he came back to town he cherished the hope that he would find Nita at the office and things would go on as before. Possibly this was only a dream. Possibly Nita was back in her cubbyhole at the *Globe*, pounding out stories.

She wasn't there. She hadn't returned to her job. The managing editor irately wanted to know what had happened to her.

"I don't know," Don Reed said. "I just don't know. All I can say is that she skipped, but don't ask me why."

With that answer the editor had to be content. He was annoyed at the loss of a valuable employee, but he was too busy a man to demand a full explanation. The other members of staff, less busy than the editor, did demand explanations. The reporter parried their questions. Answering their questions truthfully would only get him a nomination as a candidate for a nuthouse.

REED prepared to begin his search for Nita Ayer. Fortunately his job as a reporter gave him both the time for investigation and an excuse for carrying it on. Nita had rented an apartment in an apartment hotel. Reed's first step was to go there. He planned to obtain a key from the manager and make an investigation of her personal effects.

It was possible she might have left old letters, books, or something that would give him a clue about her. A frequent caller at the hotel to see Nita, Reed already knew the manager. He anticipated no difficulty in securing a key to her apartment.

"Glad to give you a key to her apartment, Reed," the manager said. "However, you understand I will have to go with you while you make your inspection."

"Of course," the reporter agreed. Nita was a tenant of the hotel and in her absence it was the manager's duty to protect her property left in the apartment. Obtaining a passkey, the manager conducted Reed to the rooms Nita had occupied.

"What happened to Miss Ayer?" the manager asked.

"Nobody knows," Reed answered. "She disappeared and we're trying to locate her. Has she, by any chance, been here recently?"

"I haven't seen her," the manager said. "Of course I might not see her for days anyway, but if she entered or left the building, the desk clerk would be almost certain to see her—and he hasn't. I happen to know because a missing tenant is always reported to me. Ah, here we are..."

Opening the door of the apartment, the manager stepped inside. Reed, following close behind, bumped into the back of a tweed suit when the manager came to an abrupt stop in front of him. An exclamation of surprise burst from the manager's lips. The reporter peered over his shoulder to see what had happened.

The room had been ransacked. It looked as if a cyclone had struck it. Contents of the dresser drawers had been brought to the living room and dumped in the middle of the floor. The drawers had been completely pulled out of the writing desk. The top had been torn off the desk, apparently in search of a suspected secret hiding place. The carpet had been pulled off the floor, the pictures taken from the wall and the brown-paper covering torn from their backs. In places the paper had been ripped from the wall, apparently in a search for something that might have been hidden behind the wallpaper. Books had been pulled from the shelves, the cushions of the sofa and chairs had been ripped open, flowerpots had been broken and the dirt dumped out on the floor.

It was the most perfect example of systematic destruction that Reed had ever seen. Nothing that might have served as a hiding place had been overlooked. Even Nita's clothing had been taken from the hangers and pulled apart seam by seam.

The manager's face hardened. "Burglars!" he gasped.

"Burglars, hell!" Reed said. He made a quick inspection of the rooms. In one spot, where the carpet had been pulled up, the wooden floor was smudged and blackened. Bits of crumbled ashes remained in this place. A small fire had been lit here, something had been burned, and then the ashes had been stamped on to remove the possibility that the experts of the police department might make something out of them. "They were burglars all right," the reporter said grimly. "But they weren't looking for money or jewels. They were looking for something they could burn, something like several sheets of paper." He pointed toward the smudged spot on the floor.

"Why should they do that?" the manager asked.

"To keep me, or somebody else, from finding them..." the reporter said bitterly. "There was information here, information that might have been of value to anyone who was looking for Nita Ayer. Somebody suspected it might be here. Somebody found it, and destroyed it. Damn me for a fool for not coming here sooner. When do you think this happened?"

"I—I have no idea," the manager faltered. "It must have been done at night, but whether it was done last night or several nights ago, I have no way of knowing. This—this an outrage. I'm going to call the police."

"Go ahead and call them," Reed said.

"If you find anything, call me at the *Globe*. But if you or the police or anybody else finds anything, I'm going to be greatly surprised." He turned and stalked from the room. Inwardly he was cursing himself for not having come right away to Nita's apartment. But he hadn't thought of it soon enough and somebody had beaten him to the punch.

Somebody—*or some thing?*

A cold wind passed over his body as the thought occurred to him that *some thing* might have searched Nita's apartment. What if the burglars had been supernatural?

Horror walked into his mind, grinned, and passed on. He shrugged the thought aside. "Supernatural or natural," he said grimly to himself. "I'm going to find out what's back of this. And I'm going to find Nita…"

The next day he took the second step in the search for Nita Ayer.

## CHAPTER SIX
*The Messenger from the Hidden World*

THE first edition of the *Globe* that hit the streets the next morning carried on its back pages a picture of Nita Ayer. Under it was the caption: NEWSPAPER WOMAN MISSING

The text that accompanied the picture carried an appeal to anyone who possessed any information as to the whereabouts of Nita Ayer to get in touch with Don Reed, care of the *Globe*.

If Reed had had his way, the picture would have appeared on the front page and would have been twice as large. The editors over-ruled his demand, arguing that since there was no evidence of foul play, the paper, to protect itself, could not carry a bigger story. The editors were not too anxious to run to the story at all but they had grudgingly permitted it to appear on the back pages. The editors thought they were being reasonable about the matter. They were concerned about Nita, but after all, she might have simply decided not to come back, in which case a wild search for her might blow up in the face of the editors, much to their chagrin. Don Reed saw their reluctance to handle the story as another illustration of the operation of an unconscious censorship.

There was one section of the paper the editors could not easily control—the paid ads appearing in the classified agony column. The reporter grimly paid his money to the ad department. This ad appeared in the personal notices.

*Missing—Nita Ayer. Where did she come from? Where is she hiding? Who is she? Reward. Don Reed, care of the* Globe.

He paid for the ad to be run one week. Somewhere was somebody who knew something about Nita Ayer. The ad, the photograph, and the story should bring to light information about her. Meanwhile, all he could do was wait for something to happen.

He didn't have to wait long. That afternoon a messenger boy came into the office with a message for him. He snatched the letter from the fingers of the boy, and tore open the envelope.

"Don—" the letter ran. "Don't be a silly fool. I'm perfectly safe, I'm happy, but I'm not coming back. I have good reasons for my actions, reasons which concern only me. You stay out of this."

The letter was signed "Nita."

The first person to answer his ad had been Nita herself! Nita was alive! If he could only believe what she said, she was safe. She was obviously in Chicago. The speed with which the ad had been answered and the fact that a messenger boy had been used to deliver the answer proved that she was in Chicago.

"Where did you get this message?"

"At my office, sir," the boy promptly answered. "The manager gave me a lot of stuff to deliver and this was in it."

"What's the telephone number of your office?"

Reed dialed the messenger service, got the manager on the phone. In his mind was the hope that Nita had left a trail behind her. If he could only trace this message. If he could find where she was hiding...

"Sorry," the manager said. "I have a record of a letter given to us to transmit to you. We keep a record of all such transactions. In this case the name and the address of the sender were not filled in."

"Is there any way you can trace the person who gave it to you?"

"None whatsoever. If the sender doesn't choose to leave his name and address, there is nothing we can do. In this case the letter was turned in at our office, the fee was paid. Our responsibility in the matter ends with delivery. Sorry I can't help you, but that's the way it is."

REED flung the phone back on its hook, tossed the boy a tip, and swore. The first clue that might have led to Nita had run straight into a stone wall.

The reason it had run into a stone wall was obvious.

Nita did not want to be found.

The reason she did not want to be found was also obvious.

She was protecting him. She had told him to forget her, that she was dangerous to him. She loved him! Therefore she was staying away from him.

More than ever he sensed the tremendous mystery back of this girl. Beautiful, enigmatic Nita Ayer! Who was she? Where had she come from? What secret was she hiding?

Cold winds passed over the reporter's body. Suddenly he remembered something Nita had told him. The *hurthen*—the only way you knew a *hurthen* was near was by a feeling of cold.

He was cold—cold! There was a coldness pressing against his spine, there was a coldness on his legs. He crouched at his desk, not moving, not daring to move. Was there an invisible *something* near him? Had a *hurthen* followed him from Wisconsin? He remembered the dog that had tried to run and, while running, had died. He remembered Merthu crouched back in the corner of his cell, trying to make himself as small as possible. He remembered the terrible fear on the face of the bronze youth. Something of that same fear was walking through Reed's mind.

He looked slowly around. The newspaper office, the battered copy desk, the city editor with his green eye-shade, re-write men banging out copy, boys hurrying to the copy desk for proofs, all this was perfectly normal. From the street outside the building came the vague tooting of auto horns, the bang of streetcars, the shouts of newsboys. In the distance there was the old, familiar rattle and bang of the elevated trains. The sights and the sounds were those of a normal afternoon in Chicago. If he walked to the window and looked down, he would see the streets crowded with people.

A reporter, coming by, stopped suddenly and looked at Reed.

"What makes, Don?" he demanded. "You look like you're seeing a ghost."

Reed forced a grin to his face. "I got a little touch of indigestion," he said.

The reporter accepted the explanation. "Take a bromo," he advised. "And change your brand of whiskey."

"Thanks," Reed said feebly. He watched the reporter walk up the hall and enter into an argument with the city editor. The sight was so perfectly normal that it nearly shocked him. Everybody on the staff argued with the city editor. It was custom, tradition. Yet among these familiar sights and scenes, Don Reed sat very still, aware only of a feeling of cold.

Was the cold feeling going away? Or was it growing stronger? He waited. In him was the fear that death was very near. What had Nita said? You might seem to die of heart failure. Or a needle might plunge through your heart. A needle had been plunged through Merthu's heart.

He waited. Slowly, an inch at a time, the cold feeling went away. It was gone. Gone! From head to foot, he was covered with sweat. He sagged back into his chair.

Even if death had been very near, even if death might come again, he knew what he was going to do. He went down to the advertising department, inserted a notice in the personal column.

"Nita: I'm playing out my hand in this game. Don."

The notice made the last edition of the paper. Somewhere in Chicago within a couple of hours Nita would buy a copy of the paper. She would know that he was not quitting, that he was not giving up. He had been dealt a hand in a strange game of hide and seek with death. Nothing short of death would keep him from playing out that hand...

When he returned to the newsroom, Don found an envelope lying on his desk. It too, had been delivered by the messenger service. He opened it. It read:

*Dear Mr. Reed:*

*The picture of Nita Ayer in the Globe has been called to my attention. If you will call at my quarters at 6163 S. Argoyle Avenue at nine o'clock tonight, it is possible that I may be able to give you some of the information you are seeking.*

*You may recall our previous meeting.*

*Sincerely yours,*

*James Randolph Harker.*

The great Harker! The man who called himself the messenger from the hidden world. Somewhere, somehow, Harker was mixed up in this mad enigma...

REED'S first stop was at the shop of a shifty-eyed pawnbroker on South State Street. There, for a price, he obtained a gun to replace the one the Wisconsin sheriff had taken from him. It was a bulldog revolver with a short barrel, one the ugliest-looking weapons ever fabricated by the human race. And at close quarters, one of the most efficient. He slipped it, and an extra supply of cartridges, into his pocket. He wondered what good a gun would be against—well, against a *hurthen*. A shudder passed over him at the thought. A gun would probably be worse than useless, but at any rate it made him feel better.

He went home, to shave and change clothes. Home to him, as it had been to Nita, as it is to thousands of others in Chicago, was an efficiency apartment in a large hotel on the near North Side. Stuffed in his mailbox at the hotel desk was a telephone slip to call his office.

"There's a package here for you," he was told over the phone.

"What kind of a package?"

"Just a package," the telephone operator at the *Globe* told him. "It's about three inches square and it's wrapped in tissue paper. Addressed to you in what looks like a girl's handwriting. I thought it might be important so I called to tell you about it."

"I'll be down to pick it up a little later," Reed said. A package for him! He had made no purchase, had ordered nothing from any store. Later, when he returned to his office and opened the package, a note fell out. The note was in Nita's handwriting.

*"Dear Don: If you are determined to play out your hand in this game there is nothing left for me to do except try to help you, but again I want to warn you that you are risking your life. Indeed, you have already risked it. Beyond question, your newspaper search for me has already been noticed, and in consequence your death, in all probability, has been decreed. Don——"* (There was a sudden, pathetic appeal in the note.) *"——I tried to warn you! Why wouldn't you listen?*

*"Go to some small hotel, register under an assumed name, and stay out of sight until you hear from me. Keep in contact with your office by telephone. I will call your office and leave a message for you. Until you hear from me, hide!*

*"Above all things, wear the object I am enclosing in this box. Frantically, Nita."*

In the box, wrapped in tissue paper, was Nita's strange moonstone bracelet. She had given him her bracelet! With a shock, he remembered her words. The bracelet was a means of protection against the *hurthen*. Merthu's bracelet had been broken. Nita had said the *hurthen* would not have been able to kill Merthu if the bracelet had not been broken.

In an effort to protect Don, she had given him her bracelet!

"The little fool!" the reporter raged. "She shouldn't have done this. She shouldn't have—" Seeing the startled eyes of the telephone operator who had given him the box, he hastily broke off. Already the whisper was going round the office that Reed had taken a dive off the deep end. There was no point in adding fresh fuel to the flame. Thanking the girl for holding the box for him, he left the building.

He had a problem to solve. Nita had told him to go into hiding. She had warned him. The problem was whether or not he was going to do what she ordered.

"Does she think I'm a sissy?" he said angrily. "Does she think I'll run and hide when somebody says 'Boo!' "

He knew what he was going to do. There had never been any doubt in his mind about what he would do. Hailing a cab, he climbed into it.

He intended to keep his appointment with Harker.

IN THE back seat of the cab, he examined the bracelet. The moonstones glistened with a milky light. The metal felt slightly warm to the touch, as though it was warmed by hidden fires. While the cab jolted south through Chicago, he examined it minutely, trying to trace the fine lines engraved in the metal, the lines that might be writing in some unknown language, and might be mere ornamentation. He could not decide whether they were ornamentation or writing. They might be either.

"That's the trouble with this damned business!" he said bitterly to himself. "Everything can always be something else. Nothing is ever clear, nothing is ever certain."

The bracelet might be a charm. In that case, the name for it would be magic. It might be a cunningly contrived scientific device, in which case the name for it would be science. And then it might be just a bracelet made to delight the heart of a woman who loved jewelry. There was no way to know what it was. The only sure fact he had was that Nita believed in it. She had worn it constantly. To which could be added the fact that she loved him enough to try to protect him at the risk of her own life. Muscles jutted into knots at the corners of his jaws at the thought.

Re-wrapping the bracelet in its protecting tissue paper, he slipped it into his pocket. He could not wear it on his wrist. Men did not wear jewelry. Wearing the bracelet would make him a marked man.

The address that Harker had given him turned out to be a large, rambling stone house located on a big lawn. It was surrounded by an iron fence. Both were relics of the days when this section of Chicago had been suburban, the builders here aspiring to create an exclusive residential section. Once fine homes had been built along these quiet streets, but the city had flowed over and around them, engulfing them in its resistless tide. When this house was new, you could be certain that the person who lived in it was a wealthy, respected citizen. Today anyone might live here.

Reed pushed the gate open, went up the brick walk. There was a light burning over the front door. He rang the bell. Almost instantly the door opened. A Negro stood there. He was a giant of a man. At least six feet six inches tall, and broad in proportion, he looked as if he could lick Joe Louis with one hand tied behind him. With the exception of a turban wrapped around his head, he was clad in the conventional black and white of a butler. Reed blinked at him. He had expected Harker to open the door. He had not expected to find a butler.

"You wish to see the master," the servant said. His voice was so deep it seemed to issue from some cavernous well.

"I came to see a man named Harker," the reporter answered. "I don't know about this 'master' angle."

"Mr. Harker is the master," the butler replied. "Are you Mr. Reed?"

"Yes."

"Enter, please. You are expected."

Bowing, the butler stepped aside. Reed entered. He heard the door close behind him. A split second later he felt the servant touch him. The touch was as light as a feather but Reed sensed what was happening. His hands leaped toward the pockets of his coat. He spun around.

In one hand the butler was holding his gun. In the other hand he held the tissue-wrapped bracelet. As Reed had entered, the servant had picked his pockets. The most expert pickpocket in Chicago could not have done a better job of it.

"Give me that," the reporter snapped.

The servant shook his head. "No guns allowed," he said. "As for this—" He was unwrapping the paper from the bracelet. "When I determine what it is, perhaps it will be returned to you. Ah—" Moonstones glowing gently, the bracelet lay in his huge palm. The servant looked at it. He seemed to freeze. A tremor passed over his body. From slitted eyes, he glanced up at Reed. The reporter lunged for the bracelet. He found himself looking into the muzzle of his own gun.

"Keep back!" the butler said. "K—keep back."

REED backed away. It was all he could do. The butler stared at him, gun held unwaveringly, and the reporter knew he was trying to make up his mind whether or not to shoot. The bracelet had scared the servant, scared him badly. He had recognized it instantly. When he looked at it, terror had walked across his face. Terror was still on his face, blind, mad terror.

With an effort of will, he seemed to regain control of himself.

"Th—the m—master will see y—you," he said. With the gun, he gestured toward a door. "In there…"

Covered by the gun, Reed opened the door. He stepped into a large comfortably furnished room. Shelves filled with books extended from floor to ceiling. On the floor was an Oriental rug, from the richness of the colors and the design, a masterpiece worth a small fortune. Soft lights cast a mellow glow over the room.

Against the farther wall was a large, antique desk. Harker was sitting behind this desk. He looked up when Reed entered the room, looked over the reporter's shoulder at the butler, his face a thundercloud.

"Samadu! You fool! What is the meaning of this? Did I not tell you I was expecting this gentleman?"

"Master," the giant whispered pleadingly. "He had a gun."

"What of it? Did you expect him not to have a gun? You fool—"

"Please, master," the giant begged. "He also had—*this!*"

He extended the hand that held the bracelet. Harker saw the bracelet for the first time.

A lightning change came over his face. All anger left it. His cheeks, puffed to shout, deflated, sagged in upon themselves. The pupils of his eyes widened. He stared at the bracelet. Terror grooved his face.

There was silence in the room. Far away, as though from another world, Reed heard the honk of an automobile horn. The sound was not repeated. Harker swallowed. Reed could see the motion of his throat. He seemed to be making an effort to regain control of himself.

He spoke. His voice was a whisper. "You may go, Samadu," he said.

Silently the servant laid the gun and the bracelet on the desk in easy reach of Harker. In silence he left the room. Harker opened a drawer of his desk. Using a ruler, he pushed the gun and the bracelet off the top of the desk. They fell into the drawer. Harker closed it. He looked up at Reed. In his eyes was more malevolence than the reporter had ever seen in the eyes of any man. Hate, vicious, bitter, burning hate, looked out of Harker's eyes.

"Well," he said. "A son of destiny…"

"What?" Reed said.

"You fooled me," Harker said. "You pulled the wool over my eyes very neatly. I thought, when I met you in that Wisconsin jail, that you were just another stupid reporter. I thought, when you advertised for information about Nita Ayer, that you were a stupid fool sticking your nose into something that did not concern you. It was very cleverly done. I did not begin to suspect your true identity."

THE reporter kept his face under control. He did not know whether he was dealing with a madman or whether, beneath Harker's gibberish, there was hidden a terrifying vein of truth.

Reed had remained standing. "May I sit down?" he asked.

"Certainly," Harker replied, nodding toward a chair.

Reed pulled up a chair and sat down. Quite calmly he lit a cigarette. "And now?" he said.

"A cool one you are," Harker said, surveying him. Suddenly there was irritation in his voice. "Why are they always so cool and calm, these fools who call themselves the sons of destiny? Why does nothing, even the threat of death, ever move them?" He pounded on his desk.

Reed shrugged. "I came here seeking information about Nita Ayer," he said.

Harker stared at him in an amazement he did not attempt to hide. "You are attempting to keep up that fiction?" he gasped. "Now that I know who you are, you still pretend that your purpose in coming here was to seek information about her?"

"Why not?"

"Why not?" Harker gasped. "Why—why—why not?" He seemed at a loss for words. There was exasperation on his face. He looked at Reed, then looked away. "Do you think I am so stupid that I will believe any story you may tell me, after—after that bracelet was found in your possession? Do—do you think you can stick to the story that you are a reporter attempting to trail a missing employee? Do you think I am that stupid?"

Reed said nothing. There was confusion in his mind, roaring confusion. When he first met Harker he had been convinced that the man was a fake, that in all probability he was the leader of some secret cult that found its followers among the lunatic fringe of the human race. Harker, with great ostentation, had said he was a messenger from the hidden world. This statement alone had branded him as a faker. His pompous manner had confirmed the impression. Yet Harker had answered his ad. Harker had either known something about Nita Ayer or had hoped to find out something. And certainly Harker had recognized Nita's bracelet, not apparently as belonging to her, but as belonging to some group that he called the "sons of destiny." Because the bracelet had been found in Reed's possession, Harker had leaped to the conclusion that the reporter belonged to this group.

What if Harker was not a faker? What if he was what he claimed to be, a messenger from the hidden world? What was the hidden world? Who were the sons of destiny?

There was confusion in Reed's mind. But through that confusion a thread of truth was beginning to run. Facts that had fitted nowhere began to slip into place. A kind of picture was beginning to emerge. The whole picture was foggy—as yet. It was blurred and out of focus. But here and there spots of light were beginning to emerge. Vaguely he sensed rather than saw a kind of dim relationship between facts that until now had appeared to be completely isolated.

Harker knew something. That was now clearly obvious. Harker thought that Reed was a member of a group that he called the sons of destiny. The obvious thing to do was to stall and try to find out what Harker knew.

Stalling was risking his life and he knew it. He shrugged the thought aside. In his mind was the grim suspicion that his life was already forfeited anyhow.

Reed grinned. "Exactly how stupid do you want me to think you?" he asked.

Harker stared at him in dumfounded amazement.

## CHAPTER SEVEN
*The Blackness Beyond the Door*

"YOU do not seem to realize where you are," Harker said slowly.

"Oh, I know where I am all right," Reed said easily. "My office knows where I am, too, and so does the police department. Naturally, I appreciated there might be some risk in coming here and made my plans accordingly. If I do not return within a reasonable time, I am afraid you will have to answer some embarrassing questions."

Reed was lying. He had informed no one of his plans. But Harker didn't know that. Any ideas of violence that the latter might hold would be tempered by the belief that Reed's whereabouts were known.

Harker said nothing. The baffled look on his face became more pronounced. There was silence in the room, complete silence, the utter absence of any sound. It suddenly struck Reed that the friendly sounds of the city night, the clang of streetcar bells, the honk of automobile horns, were no longer audible. Chicago seemed to have gone to sleep.

Harker shook his head. "I do not begin to understand it," he said, and Reed got the impression that his inability to understand was somehow making the man afraid. Harker reminded him of a man who suspects a trap but can't see the snare.

"What is so difficult to understand?" the reporter asked.

"The fact that you would put yourself in my power," Harker answered. He looked at Reed, a worried frown on his face. "You see, I am being frank," he said, spreading his hands. "That you, a son of destiny, should put yourself in my power when you *must* know what I am, is unbelievable. The only logical answer is that I am being tricked, that a trap is being set for me, and that somehow you are the bait of that trap."

"Ah!" said Reed. So his impression that Harker was afraid of a trap had been correct. But what kind of a trap was it that he feared?

"Why did you answer my ad if there was a chance you would be trapped?" the reporter asked.

"When I answered your advertisement, I thought you were a nosey reporter inquiring into something that did not concern you. It was my intention to fill you full of hot air and to further the conviction you had gained at our first meeting, namely, that I was a faker. Believe me, I did not suspect your true identity, or I would have handled the matter in an entirely different manner."

Grim, harsh tones crept into his voice. He looked at Reed and lights guttered in his eyes, lights of hate. There was no mistaking his meaning. A shiver passed over the reporter.

"I take it you mean I would have been rubbed out?" he said, keeping his voice calm.

"You take it correctly," Harker said grimly. "Rubbed out is a mild expression for what would have happened to you…"

"What long teeth you have, grandmother," Reed said. "If I may ask it, why all this sudden tendency to homicide? Don't you like the sons of destiny, or do you just enjoy bumping people off?"

Harker looked at the reporter. There was a thoughtful look in his eyes. "What a stupid question," he said slowly. A worried frown creased his forehead. "Or is it so stupid?" he spoke. "Is it possible—*could it be possible*—that you are not a son of destiny? No…it's not possible. You have the power bracelet of the sons and daughters of destiny. That means you are one of them. But—" A worried, fearful tone crept into his voice. "—could you have come into possession of the bracelet in some other manner? Could you have found it or could it have been given to you…?"

FIST crashing on his desk, Harker leaped to his feet. "By the devil, it is possible!" he shouted. "The bracelet belongs to the girl! She is in love with you. She knows you are in danger. She gave you her bracelet, to protect you. You are *not* a son of destiny. You don't know a thing about—about us. For the last hour, you've been sitting there trying to pump information out of me—*out of me*…"

Harker nearly screamed the words. The idea that anyone would try to get information out of him seemed to enrage him. He pounded on the desk. In his fury he knocked a heavy inkwell to the floor. Reed picked it up.

"You seem to have analyzed the situation very accurately," he said. "Try your analysis on this…"

With all his strength, he flung the inkwell in the other's face. Made of glass, the inkwell weighed two or three pounds. It hit with a solid *thud*. It was too heavy to break. Ink splashed in every direction. Harker reeled backward. He crashed against the wall, slid to the floor, made gasping sounds in his throat.

Reed jerked open the desk drawer, grabbed his gun and the bracelet. A glance told him that Harker was likely to be unconscious for several minutes, but there remained the possibility that Samadu, waiting in the entrance hall, had heard the crash. Gun ready, the reporter faced the door. He expected the servant to put in an appearance any second. He waited. Samadu did not come. Either he had not heard the crash or he had strict orders not to interrupt Harker no matter what happened.

"I gotta get out of here," Reed whispered to himself. "I gotta get out of here—*fast.*"

There was danger in this room, deadly danger. He did not understand the nature of the danger, but he clearly sensed its existence. Harker was no faker. Harker, whoever he really was, possessed incredible powers. Reed knew he had been lucky to catch the man off-guard. When Harker recovered consciousness—the reporter shuddered. A cold sweat was popping out all over his body. He tiptoed to the door and listened…

No sound came from the hallway. If Samadu was there, he was keeping quiet. Reed's plan was simple. Jerk open the door, cover Samadu with the gun, force the servant to open the front door and to march ahead of him out of the house. Once on the street, he could grab a cab, get the hell away from here. In seclusion, he could plan his next move. First of all he had to get out of this house, out of this room, if he wanted to continue living. Harker's threats had been too clear for him to doubt the man's intentions.

He took a deep breath, jerked open the door. He was poised to hurl himself through the opening. He looked outward, ready to leap—and caught himself. Terror gripped his heart.

Beyond the open door was—*blackness!* It was not the darkness that comes when the lights are turned off, not the darkness of a shuttered room at midnight, but an utter, complete blackness that gave back no sign of light. It was such a blackness as was on the void before the heavens were lifted up, before the earth was set in place, before the sun and the stars came. There was no glimmer of light in it. It was not just a hallway without lights. It was tangible blackness.

Fighting the panic in his heart, Reed stared at it. As he watched, little streamers seemed to detach themselves from the void of darkness, to come like exploratory fingers into the room. Like the tongue of a snake, they reached toward him. Then he saw a glowing, ethereal image appear in the blackness. Reed raised his arm in fear. The image did likewise. He let out a gasp as he realized that the image was somehow his own, like a ghostly reflection. Within the image was a skeletal image. He slammed the door and ran to the window. Whatever was in that hallway, one thing was certain: escape through it was dangerous. That left the windows. He ripped aside the heavy drapes, unlocked the window, flung it up—and looked out into the same kind of blackness that had been in the hall!

BEYOND the window lay darkness. There was no glimmer of any kind of light. The streetlights were not visible, nor was the sky. He could not see the street, the lawn, or the shrubbery on the lawn. There was only blackness and silence, a silence so great it hurt his eardrums. Suddenly he remembered how, a little while before, the familiar sounds of the city had seemed to fade away into the distance, to go into silence, how the clang of the street car bells had died down, how the honk of automobile horns had died into nothingness. Had this blackness come then? He could not hear a sound. And, exploratory fingers of darkness were coming through the open window. He slammed it shut.

There were other exits, another door, other windows. He needed only a few minutes to try them all. At the end he knew the horrible truth, beyond each door, beyond each window, was nothing but darkness. Grimly he struck a match, opened the hall door, and tossed the match into the darkness. Its little flame was swallowed up, was instantly gone into nothingness.

Cold chills were shuddering through his body; even colder winds were screaming through his mind. He pulled a book from the shelf, tossed it through the open door, waited for the sound of it striking the floor to come back to his straining ears, like a man caught in a dark cave who finds a drop-off yawning beneath his feet and tosses a pebble outward so that the sound of the pebble will tell him how deep is the cavern ahead of him. No sound returned!

Either the blackness deadened sound or there was no bottom to the pit that yawned outside the door. The reporter fought off panic. He closed the door. A sound behind him jerked his head around. Harker had made the sound. Harker had recovered consciousness. Harker was watching him.

"Why don't you run?" Harker asked softly. "I won't stop you. Jerk the door open and run."

Reed licked his lips. The salt of the perspiration on his face was acid on his tongue. "No, thank you," he said. "I believe I'll stay right here. What—what is on the other side of that door?"

Harker pulled a handkerchief out of his breast pocket, wiped ink from his face. "Nothing," he said.

"N—nothing?"

"You heard me. Nothing. Not anything. The void. There's absolutely no matter, at least as you know matter, no space—nothing." Harker straightened his chair, sat down heavily in it. There was an ugly bruise on his forehead. In his eyes was black hatred. "How would you like to die?" he said, looking at Reed.

There was no mistaking the subtle menace in Harker's voice. The reporter swallowed. "I don't know," he said. "What kind of deaths do you have handy?"

Harker looked startled. "May I be damned if you're not a cool one," he said.

"Ice-water-Reed is what they call me," the reporter said. His hand was in his pocket on the gun. He was stalling for time, his mind racing desperately as it sought a solution for his problem. He could not escape. Beyond this room lay darkness. Harker somehow controlled that darkness. If he could force the man to lift the blackness—like a drowning man, he was grasping for straws and he knew it. Straws were the only things within his reach. It was grasp them or grasp nothing.

Harker grunted. "This is no time for stalling," he said. He snapped his fingers. "Look…"

"Look where?" Reed asked lightly. The words froze on his lips. Directly in front of his eyes something was hanging in the air. It was gray and indistinct but he could clearly make out the outlines—a thin, narrow streak of grayness, pointed like a spear, aimed straight at him.

"W—what is that?" Reed husked.

Harker smiled almost imperceptibly and said, "Did you ever see a *hurthen?*"

"N—no!"

"Well, you're seeing one now. Very useful creatures, the *hurthen.* They make excellent body-guards and first-class executioners." Harker chuckled under his breath. He seemed to be enjoying himself. "It has been here all the time, watching you, needing only my order to attack. I knew you could not see it until I made it visible but I wondered why you did not feel it. Hah! How would you like to have that needle-pointed spear driven straight through your heart?"

REED did not, could not, answer. Again that terrible feeling of cold was creeping over him. Somehow the gray creature radiated coldness. Or perhaps it drew heat from the surrounding air, with the result that anyone near it felt cold. Looking closely at it, he could barely see two tiny unwinking eyes and he knew that the creature somehow was alive. It possessed intelligence, a horrible intelligence. But more than anything else, it possessed malevolence, hate. It hated him. It hated all living things. It would like to destroy him. He could well imagine how one of these things, loose in a chicken house, would destroy the whole flock. It seemed to be yearning toward him, to be quivering with eagerness to get at him.

"Now that you can see it, how do you like it?" Harker asked.

Reed tried to speak and choked.

"I see you don't like it any more than Merthu did," Harker observed. "Or any of the others who had the misfortune of seeing it."

"This—this killed Merthu?" Reed whispered.

"Yes," Harker gloated. "I went there for the express purpose of killing him. The first *hurthen*, which was sent as soon as it was certain he had arrived, failed in its task. They are not, you conceive, too reliable when distant from their masters. They sometimes stray, and being bloodthirsty little beasts, will wander around attacking both men and animals. I think the first one was distracted from its mission by other prey although it is of course possible that some strength remained in Merthu's bracelet of power, thus thwarting the *hurthen*. I went personally to attend to the matter," He chuckled. "And I almost succeeded in trapping the girl at the same time. Oh yes, that murder charge almost took care of Miss Ayer. It was too bad that she escaped."

"Yes," said Reed grimly. "It sure was too bad." The dryness in his voice did not reveal the hot tension in his mind. At last he knew that Nita had not killed Merthu. Harker had done that little job! Harker and the gray creature that hung in the air before him...

"Are you ready?" Harker asked playfully, like a cat with a mouse. He was teasing the reporter, and he seemed to be enjoying his little torture.

"If you're ready, I am," Reed said huskily. "But I warn you—" The gun leaped from his pocket. "—if that gray monstrosity moves toward me, you're a dead man. It may be able to float in the air, but the question is, can it move faster than a bullet? No, the bullet won't be aimed at it. I doubt if a bullet would harm it. The slug will go through your guts, Harker. *Keep your hands in sight and don't move.*"

HARKER had started to rise. He hastily settled back in his chair when the muzzle of the gun covered him.

"You forgot I might have taken my gun from your desk while you were unconscious, didn't you?" Reed said. "Well, don't forget this: If you make a move I don't like, I'll put a bullet through you. If that thing," he gestured toward the *hurthen*, "moves a fraction of an inch, you'll get the same treatment. Put your hands on the top of the desk and keep them there."

Slowly Harker put his hands on the desk. The *hurthen* did not move. Reed was intently watching it out of the corners of his eyes. It hung motionless in the air, waiting the command of its master to go into action.

"I want to ask some questions," the reporter said. "Who are you?"

Harker did not answer.

"Speak up!" the reporter grated. "Or by all that's holy—" His fingers tightened around the gun, emphasizing his meaning.

"I scarcely think you will find it advisable to shoot," Harker spoke. "If you kill me, you will still find some slight difficulty in escaping from this room. To be alone here with my little friend," he nodded toward the motionless *hurthen*, "would not be exactly pleasant. No, Reed, you won't shoot me. You might as well put that gun down because you're not going to use it."

"I'm not?" the reporter said.

"No. I can think of more pleasant ways to commit suicide. This room is suspended in nothingness, Reed, and only I can release the nothingness. If you shoot me, you will stay here forever. Only, of course, my little friend will soon take care of you if I were gone."

"Will your little friend..." Reed reached into his pocket. "...be able to overcome this?"

He held Nita's bracelet up for Harker to see. The bracelet of power, Harker had called it. The reporter did not begin to know how to use it, but he knew, from the way Harker had spoken about it and from what Nita had told him, that somehow tremendous powers were leashed within that circlet of carved metal and moonstones. Harker looked startled when he saw it. His eyes darted toward the desk drawer, then came up to fix themselves on Reed's face. There was fear in them now.

Reed clamped the bracelet on his left wrist. He rose to his feet, quickly extended his arm toward the motionless *hurthen*. As the bracelet came toward it, the gray creature leaped away. It lunged against the wall of the room like a frightened bird that does not know where it is going but seeks only to escape. Recovering from striking the wall, it darted toward the ceiling, where, in a corner of the room, it hung quivering, as far away from the bracelet as it could get.

Reed chuckled. "Your little friend seems frightened," he observed.

Harker looked at him from bulging eyes. "W—what are you going to do?" he whispered.

"I'm going to take a walk," the reporter answered.

"A w—walk?"

"Yes. You surely know how to walk. You put one foot ahead of the other and pretty soon you find you have traveled from one place to another. Get up, Harker. I wouldn't think of taking a walk without the pleasure of your company."

"M—me?"

"Yes, you!" Reed snapped. "You will walk ahead of me. You will open the door and step into that blackness on the other side. Of course," the reporter shrugged, "if you should find such a step unpleasant to contemplate, and should cause the blackness to go away—"

He didn't finish but Harker understood his meaning. As long as the blackness waited outside the room, Reed knew he could not escape. Harker controlled that blackness. He controlled Harker. If he forced Harker to step through the door—

"I—I won't do it…" Harker gulped.

"If you don't," Reed said grimly, "I'll put a soft-nosed bullet through your guts. Then we'll stay here and watch each other die. You'll die first, Harker. With you dead, I'll see whether the darkness remains. Which will it be, Harker—a walk, or a bullet?"

The ink from the inkwell had splashed all over Harker's face and had partly dried. It was dissolving now, as sweat popped out of the pores of his skin. Sweaty ink was running down his cheeks as he stared at Reed.

"I don't suppose I need to remind you that I mean what I say?" the reporter said.

"N—no," Harker said. He rose to his feet, walked around the desk and toward the door. The reporter, gun jammed in his back, followed him. What would happen when the door opened? Would the blackness that Harker said was nothing begin to creep into the room? If it did, Reed would know his bluff had failed.

Harker opened the door. Before him, an inky curtain of nothingness, the blackness stretched. He made a strange movement with his hands, spoke jumbled words deep in his throat. Like a veil that is torn aside, the blackness disappeared. The entrance hall with its dim lights gleaming, stood clearly revealed. The hall was empty.

"Out the front door," Reed said. "And remember—no breaks. I don't know who or what you are, Harker, but I know this much: if you make a break, I'll shoot you like I would a mad dog."

"W—where are you taking me?" Harker quavered.

"Wait and see," Reed answered. He knew exactly what he was going to do. Slipping the gun into his pocket, but keeping Harker covered, Reed forced the man to walk out to the street. He glanced back, once, at the rambling old house. To the casual eye, it looked like a perfectly ordinary old home that had gone to seed. But Reed knew that never again would he be able to regard it, or any other house, with a casual eye. Strange things happened in houses and strange things happened on earth. He whistled for a cab.

AN HOUR later the two men were in a room in a third rate hotel in the Chicago Loop. They had stopped in a drug store long enough for Reed to secure a roll of adhesive tape. Harker was sitting in a chair. His arms were taped together behind him and his legs were taped to the legs of the chair. He had, in spite of the tape, managed to recover some of his composure.

"Well, what are you going to do now?" he challenged.

"For about the first time in my life, I'm going to take some advice," the reporter answered. "I was told to hole up in a hotel and wait until a certain young lady gets in touch with my office. I'm going to do that. And when Nita Ayer calls, Harker, I'm going to turn you over to her and see what happens. I don't know for certain but I have a hunch she will be greatly interested in you, Harker; and no doubt you are interested in her. When I get you two together, there is a chance that some of this damned mystery may be cleared up."

"Y—you—" Harker choked. "Y—you're going to turn me over to Nita Ayer?" In his voice was subdued horror.

Reed smiled grimly. He surveyed the consternation on the man's face. "Does that jab you in the quick?" he asked. "Well, well. How interesting…"

## CHAPTER EIGHT
### *The Sons of Destiny*

REED, catnapping on the bed and calling his office at hourly intervals to find out if Nita had as yet left a telephone number for him to dial, spent a miserable night. His only consolation was that Harker was even more miserable. The reporter had halfway hoped that misery might loosen Harker's tongue, but not once during the night did the man break his self-imposed silence. Nor did Harker sleep. He seemed to be engrossed in his own thoughts. Meanwhile he waited.

At seven o'clock, Reed again called his office and was informed that there was no message from Nita. After making certain that Harker was securely tied, Reed taped the man's mouth shut to keep him from calling for help, then went out for breakfast. The sleepy night clerk looked at him as he went out but gave no sign of recognition. In this hotel they never asked questions.

On the street outside, Chicago was coming to life. Traffic arteries, pumping blood to the heart of the city, were beginning to quicken their beat. The streets, almost deserted overnight, were starting to take on animation.

The tides of life were flowing into the heart of the city; at dusk they would flow out again, in a great rhythm.

Reed went into a small breakfast cafe; he ate slowly.

"Coffee and a sweet roll to go," he told the waiter.

That was for Harker.

Returning to the hotel, he stopped in a drug store and bought a razor and blades. Then he went back to his room. Harker was patiently waiting for him. The man had not moved.

"Want some breakfast?" the reporter asked, removing the tape from the man's mouth and freeing one arm enough for Harker to feed himself. Harker nodded. He ate the sweet roll and drank the coffee in silence. Reed stared at him in growing wonder.

Shaving in the bathroom, Reed watched Harker through the open door. The man was quietly drinking coffee. When he finished, he sat the empty cup on the table, leaning forward in the chair so that his half-free arm would reach the table. Then he resumed his original position.

The oddity of the situation struck Reed forcibly. Through the open windows of the bathroom he could hear sparrows chirping, he could hear the rattle and the bang of the awakening city. Everything was just exactly as it had always been on a morning in Chicago. Down on the streets thousands of people were hurrying to work. Here in the bathroom he was shaving, the most commonplace occupation imaginable. In the other room, clearly visible through the open door, the most mysterious man he had ever met was sitting.

If the people of Chicago, the kids rushing to play, the mammas shaking table cloths over the back porch, the papas on the way to work, knew that a man who possessed Harker's powers existed among them, there would be the damnedest stir the world had ever seen. But they didn't know about Harker. They didn't know that such a person existed. And Reed knew that if he rushed down to the street and cornered the first person he met and tried to tell him about Harker, the man would think he had met a lunatic. If Reed tried to print the story in his paper, the only result would be that the managing editor would advise him to take a nice long vacation. Not even his reputation as a reporter would get the true story about Harker past the editors.

What—the thought struck him—was Harker's true story. Who was the man? What was he? Was Harker—his mind fumbled with the thought and almost refused it—was Harker *human?* Or, as many of the old legends said, did strange monsters go upon the earth in human form?

Of the millions in Chicago, no one else might believe in Harker. Reed believed in him. He had seen the *hurthen* hanging motionless in the air, he had seen the black wall of nothingness barring the exit from the man's study, he had heard Harker talk, weirdly, of the sons of destiny, he had seen the fear on the man's face when he saw what he called the bracelet of power.

Who and what was Harker? Reed did not know the answer to these questions. Somewhere there was an answer. He would find it. He had flung himself headfirst into a mystery madder than any ever conceived by the mind of man; grimly he intended to plow through to a solution. The answer would come in its own good time. In the meantime, he continued shaving.

THE telephone rang. He almost jerked the instrument off the wall getting to it. It was his office. "Your little chickadee called," a man's gruff voice said. "She left a number for you to call. Regent 0-8491. Hey, Don, what makes with this business anyhow? What are you after? Give out with the information, will you? What's all this funny stuff about?"

"Get off the wire," Reed growled. "I got no time to waste on you." He recognized the voice as belonging to one of the re-write men on the staff. Muttering, the rewrite man hung up.

Reed frantically dialed the number he had been given. He heard the phone ring on the other end, waited for an answer. The phone rang again and again. His blood pressure climbed higher each time it rang. Suppose no one answered? Suppose something had happened to Nita? Suppose—

The receiver clicked. "Hello," a cool, clear voice said over the wire.

"Nita…" Don shouted. Nita was on the phone. He would recognize her voice anywhere. He had found her— or she had found him. Whichever it was, it didn't matter. The only fact that mattered was that he was talking to her.

She laughed and to Don Reed her laughter had in it the musical quality of the tinkle of silver bells. "Don! You sound as excited as a schoolboy. How are you, and how are things?"

"I'm fine and things are fine and how are you?" He was a little breathless. After the agony of waiting, the pain of searching, he had found Nita.

"I'm first rate. Where are you?"

"In a hotel. Nita, when can I see you? I've got a million things to ask you."

There was a little silence. When she spoke her voice had somehow changed. "Are you sure you want to ask those questions, Don?"

Reed caught the change in her voice, the hesitancy with which she spoke.

"Nita," he said quietly, "I want to ask those questions and I want them answered. Do you understand? I've got to have them answered. I've seen too much not to have the whole story. I'll go nuts if I don't understand this business. I don't want any more stalling from you, for any reason. Are you going to answer my questions?"

THE wire was silent. Then Nita spoke. "Yes, Don. I will answer your questions, to the best of my ability. I was only making certain that you wanted an answer. Some— some persons who asked, didn't really want an answer."

"I can understand that," he said dryly.

"You have to have a tough mind to listen to the answers to those questions. I think you have a tough mind, Don. Otherwise I wouldn't tell you what you want to know, even now. This is strong medicine, too strong to give you over the telephone. Can you come to see me, Don?" She gave him an address on the west side.

"Of course I can come to see you," he said emphatically. Then he hesitated. This was the time for the explosion. He carefully sought for words to phrase what he wanted to say. "Do you mind if I bring a pal along?"

He kept his voice casual, as though he was asking a slight favor.

"A pal along?" Nita said sharply. "Don, have you taken leave of your senses? Of course you can't bring anyone else with you. What I have to tell you is for your ears alone..."

"But this is different. I'm sort of responsible for this man just at present. Besides—"

He already knew that she was a girl who could make up her mind and keep it made up. He also suspected she was not likely to let him bring anyone else along. Her "No!" rattled the telephone receiver.

"Well, okay," he said. "But Harker is going to be mighty lonely until I get back."

There was a moment of silence. He could hear her catch her breath. "Don!" she spoke sharply. "What was that name you mentioned? What was it?"

"Harker," the reporter answered. "A fellow by the name of James Randolph Harker. At least that's the name he gave me, but he may have some others that I don't know about—"

"What do you know about Harker?" she interrupted.

"Nothing much. I went out to see him last night—"

*"You went to see him?"*

"Sure. He answered my ad about you. He said he could give me some dope— What's the matter, Nita? What are you so excited about?"

She sounded frantic. "Don, where are you? Quickly where are you?"

"At a Loop hotel."

"Oh...you're all right then. For a moment I was afraid— But if you're in a hotel by yourself, you're safe enough. Don, do you mean to say that you located Harker and interviewed him last night?"

"Sure."

"Oh, you...you shouldn't have done it! You should have gone straight to some hotel and stayed there until I got in touch with you."

Listening, the reporter had the impression that she was not thinking clearly. She was telling him that he should not have gone to see Harker, but she did not seem to realize that he had offered to bring Harker with him. Her great concern at the moment seemed to be for his safety. Once she realized he was safe she then remembered the entirety of what he had said.

Then she went completely frantic.

"Don!" she almost screamed the words. "Did you say you wanted to bring Harker with you?"

"That's right."

"Then he's with you...now?"

"Right again."

He got the impression she winced then, as though she had been struck. "I'll get there as quickly as I can, Don. Maybe I'll be in time to save you—" She started to hang up.

"Hey, wait a minute," he yelled.

"But you don't understand. If Harker is with you, you're life is in danger. Every second counts—"

"I don't believe Harker will harm me."

"No?" There was extreme doubt in her voice, as though she was hearing things she did not believe.

"No. Somehow or other Harker got mixed up with some adhesive tape. It's wrapped all around his legs and his arms. I don't know exactly how it happened but I don't really believe he can even walk. As for harming me—"

"Do you mean to tell me that you've got Harker tied up?"

"Well...yes...he *is* tied up—and I supplied the tape that tied him."

*"He's a prisoner?"*

"You might put it that way."

"Don Reed, I'll never forgive you for playing with me like this. Are you honestly holding that man a prisoner?"

"That's what I'm trying to tell you, kitten. I've got him tied up and I've got a gun. I've faithfully promised him I'll blow a hole through him if he as much as bats an eyelash— "

"I'll be there as soon as I can get there," Nita cut in. With a bang, the receiver slammed down on the hook.

REED meditatively hung up his receiver. He looked at Harker. "The little girl is on her way," he said. "Anything you got on your mind that you would like to get off before she gets here?"

"Must you turn me over to her?" Harker whispered. "Isn't there something you want? Wouldn't you like to have money, or fame—"

"The man is offering bribes," Reed murmured, in mock surprise. "How much, Harker, a million?"

"Two million, if you ask it," Harker was sweating now. "Name your price. I'll pay it. And you need not think I can't pay off. I can. I can give you anything—"

"Well I'll be damned. You really must be afraid of her!"

"I'm not afraid of her. It's those she will bring with her that I fear."

"Ah! I take it she will not come alone?"

"You can be certain she won't come alone. Listen to reason, Reed. Anything you want, I'll give you. All you have to do is take this tape off arid let me get out before she gets here. You can say I escaped. She will believe you. She only halfway believes you are holding me prisoner anyhow and if you say I managed to work the tape loose, slugged you, and escaped, she won't doubt that you are telling the truth. I'll give you anything you want— millions—" The man was almost inarticulate.

The reporter shrugged. "No, thanks," he said.

"You—you won't take my offer?"

"I doubt if you could deliver on all these millions you are promising. Anyhow, Harker, it's worth a million to me to see what's going to happen to you when Nita Ayer gets here. I've got more curiosity than sense. And I'm very curious about you, and about a lot of other things. I want to know who you are and what you are doing here. I want to know where you got those strange powers you possess. I want to know what is back of you, and most of all, I want to know what kind of madness is loose in what I had once regarded—up to now—as a sensible, explainable world. No, Harker, money wouldn't satisfy my curiosity. Ah...but how did she get here so quickly?"

Steps had sounded in the hall outside. There was the sharp rap, rap, rap of high heels on the floor, such a sound made by a girl going somewhere in a hurry. The doorknob rattled and when the locked door did not open, there was a sharp rap on the panels, and a voice saying, "Don? Open up."

REED opened the door. Nita Ayer came into the room. Behind her, walking silently but with a kind of alertness that somehow reminded the reporter of plainclothes detectives closing in around a dangerous criminal, came two men. One was plainly, almost shabbily, dressed; he was wearing a threadbare brown suit. Half his face was shaved. Bits of lather clung to the uncut whiskers on the other half. He looked as if he had been suddenly interrupted, in the midst of shaving, by a message so urgent he could not wait to complete his toilet. The second man looked prosperous. He was well dressed in a smart business suit. From his appearance he might have been a broker, or an executive in a successful firm. As they entered the room, each of the men glanced once at the reporter, giving him a quick, measuring look, then paid him no further attention. Like two pointers who have suddenly scented a covey of quail, they looked quickly at Harker. When once they had looked at him, they did not look away. Nor did either of them take his right hand out of his coat pocket.

"Don!" Nita gasped. "You—you really have got him?"

"You got here mighty quickly," the reporter irrelevantly observed.

"We—we came the short way," the girl answered. She was madly excited, and more than a little frightened, though she was obviously trying to hide the latter emotion.

Reed raised his eyebrows but he did not ask what she meant by "the short way." No doubt, when she left the cell in the Wisconsin jail, she had taken the short way out. This was a question that could be answered later. Instead he nodded toward the two men. "Who are your pals?" he asked.

"They work with me. The one in brown is John Schultz. The other is James Adams. Don, I can't begin to tell you what a wonderful thing you have done in capturing this man for us." She seemed disinclined to talk further about her companions.

"Ah, yes," Reed said. "Schultz and Adams. Nice names. They would not by any chance be..." He paused. "...sons of destiny, would they?"

He did not know what reaction he expected to get, if any, but he got plenty. Nita's eyes widened in startled surprise. Adams spoke sharply to Schultz. "You take care of that. I'll watch Harker." Schultz turned quickly to the reporter. With his hand thrust in his coat pocket, he spoke loudly to Reed.

"Why do you call us that?"

Reed grinned. "What is there to get so excited about?" he drawled.

"Never mind that. Answer my question."

The reporter shrugged. "I still don't see why you should get so excited about it, but if you must know, Harker used the term. He seemed very much afraid of what he called the sons of destiny and since he was just offering me more millions than I could count not to turn him over to you, I thought you might belong to this mysterious organization."

Schultz looked a little relieved, but only a little. "Harker told you?" he demanded.

"Yes."

There was still doubt on the half-shaved face. He looked at Nita. "Do you vouch for this man?" he said nodding toward Reed.

"Yes. I vouch for him," the girl answered quickly. "You surely don't doubt him, do you? After all, he captured Harker."

Schultz was still not satisfied. "Well, if you can vouch for him, I suppose he's all right. I know he captured Harker. That's one of the things I like least. It happens to be impossible for him to have captured Harker." He shook his head.

"Hey, what do you mean?" Reed demanded.

"Let's get out of here," Schultz said. "There's something rotten about this business. I can smell it. Cut that tape off Harker, Adams, and let's take him away from here while we have a chance."

THE two men seemed to work together as a perfect team. Adams had guarded Harker while Schultz questioned Reed. Now Schultz guarded the man while Adams slit the tape that bound Harker to the chair. He worked swiftly. Harker obviously wasn't enjoying the situation. His eyes darted constantly from Schultz to Adams. He looked like a trapped rat who sees two executioners approach and does not know from which will come the fatal blow. Harker seemed to have no doubt that the blow was coming. Reed might have felt sorry for the man if he had not remembered Merthu and the way the bronze youth had tried to shrink into the corner of his cell. The reporter also remembered the *hurthen*, with which Harker had menaced him. Whatever happened to Harker, he had it coming. Obviously some grim drama of transgress and retribution was here nearing its end. Harker was on the retribution end and he didn't like it.

Reed turned to the girl. "What's biting Schultz?" he asked. "He seems to doubt me."

Nita's face was white. She kept glancing at Harker and glancing away as though she too, sensed the coming retribution and was frightened. "It isn't that Schultz doubts you," she answered. "He knows Harker's powers and— What's the matter with you?"

Reed, looking over her shoulder, saw the door open. Nita did not see it open but she saw the change in Reed's face.

In the open door stood—Samadu! The menacing giant who had served as Harker's butler...

Samadu.

As silently as he had opened it, he closed the door behind him. In his right hand, he held, no bigger than an agate taw, a ball of cut crystal. Lights were glimmering in its facets and somewhere deep within its frozen depths little hammers seemed to be striking tiny bells that gave off a continuous, angry ringing. The room was suddenly full of the sound. It beat from the ceiling, from the floors, from the walls.

Reed's hand dived for the pistol in his pocket. He did not know how Samadu had gotten here but the giant's presence could have only one meaning—disaster. He grabbed for the snub-nosed pistol in his pocket.

His arm wouldn't move. He was suddenly aware that little tingling pains were racing through his body in rhythm to the ringing of the bells held in Samadu's hand. The startling thought was in his mind that the crystal the giant was holding was somehow keeping him from moving. He fought the thought of it. It could not, must not, be true. He tried to force his hand into his pocket, so he could use the gun.

His arm wouldn't move. He tried bringing his hand up in front of his eyes to see what the devil was wrong with it. It wouldn't come up. He tried to lunge at Samadu, but heavy weights seemed to be fastened to his feet. In his mind it was clear he was somehow being held motionless.

Nita, who standing in front of him, was also frozen motionless. Schultz and Adams, busy with Harker, had suddenly ceased their effort. Angrily the bells were ringing. On Samadu's black face was the ghost of a triumphant smile.

Suddenly there was a burst of laughter in the room, triumphant laughter. Harker laughing.

"Why don't you move?" Harker was jeering. "You sons of destiny, you self-styled watchmen of the night, why don't you do something? Why don't you destroy me? Why do you stand there like fools who have turned to stone?" Again the laughter boomed forth. No one moved.

Schultz and Adams were expressionless but on Nita's face was horror.

"They find it difficult to move while the bells are ringing, eh, Samadu?" Harker said, smiling at his servant. "Something about the sound of the bells seems to keep them from moving…"

The servant grinned. "Yes, master," he said.

Harker laughed softly. He seemed to think he was watching the most wonderful joke in the world.

"Well, done, Samadu," he gloated.

"You followed my instructions perfectly and we have succeeded in trapping three of our enemies."

REED'S mind reeled at the implication back of those words. They had been trapped. Harker had planned the whole thing. He had analyzed Reed perfectly and had permitted himself to be caught, knowing that Reed would turn him over to Nita Ayer. Thus Nita and those who came with her could be lured into a trap. Harker had been using Reed as a tool. Harker, when he had offered bribes to the reporter to release him, had been putting on an act designed to convince Reed of his desire to escape. He hadn't wanted to escape. He had wanted Nita and the others to come to him, so that Samadu, who had no doubt been lurking nearby, could put in an appearance.

They had been tricked. They had been trapped. Schultz, in his dim suspicions, had been right. Reed saw the whole picture. It was a horrible picture. It swiftly became even a more horrible picture. He was aware that Harker, who somehow seemed to be immune to the paralyzing force flowing from the crystal, was patting him on the back.

"Well done, Reed," Harker was saying. "You cooperated splendidly with me. I'll make certain you're well rewarded. Your assistance was invaluable. Without you, the girl and the two men would never have come here."

Harker was saying that Reed had willingly helped him. It was a foul and monstrous lie without a word of truth in it. The reporter opened his mouth to call Harker a liar. His mouth wouldn't come open. There was a horrible choking feeling in his throat. He couldn't speak.

He glanced at Nita, begging her with his eyes not to believe Harker. She looked away. He glanced at Schultz and Adams. They looked straight back at him. They couldn't speak but in their eyes was burning bitterness.

Reed choked. Nita, Schultz, and Adams believed he had aided Harker in trapping them. He couldn't defend himself, he couldn't shout that Harker was a liar. He couldn't open his mouth. He couldn't speak.

Again Harker was patting him on the back. "Splendidly done, Reed. They didn't even begin to guess, did they? That you were working with me all the time? Look at them, Reed. Don't they look annoyed now that they know you are one of my co-workers? The girl, especially, doesn't she look hot at the way we tricked her? Those newspaper ads fooled her completely, didn't they? She thought you were honestly trying to get in touch with her because you loved her. She didn't know that you inserted those ads, knowing she would answer them, to help me trap her. A wonderful job you did, Reed. A wonderful job."

*Slap, slap, slap,* went Harker's hand on the reporter's back. Reed was aware of a whisper in his ear. "This is my revenge on you, fool, for trying to meddle in my business.

The girl you love thinks you're a traitor—how's that for revenge?"

*Slap, slap, slap* went Harker's hand on the reporter's back.

## CHAPTER NINE
### *Harker's Offer*

WHILE the hammers beat in the crystal Samadu was holding, Harker made a swift but thorough search of the three. From Adams' right coat pocket, and also from Schultz, he removed pistols. The guns did not seem to interest him. He tossed them contemptuously on the bed. From Adams' vest pocket he removed something that did interest him, greatly—a large gold watch. Eagerly he screwed off the back of the watch.

"Ah!" he said, glimpsing what was inside. "So your power bracelet was made into a watch... I suspected as much. Too bad, wasn't it," he jeered, "that the radiations from the crystal kept you from using your power? Of course, if you had gotten to your watches, and adjusted them so that they cancelled the radiations from the crystal, it would have been a different story, wouldn't it? But you couldn't move... Isn't it remarkable that for the lack of the ability to move your hand as little as six inches—far enough to reach into your vest pocket—you have come to grief?"

Harker seemed immensely proud of himself. Teasing his helpless victims, he was enjoying himself hugely. Neither Adams nor Schultz showed any emotion whatsoever. They seemed not even to hear the man. Harker finished his search with Nita. From her purse he removed a bracelet.

"How nice of you to give me this, my dear!" he gloated. He eyed her appraisingly and for the first time he seemed to become conscious of her beauty. He smacked his lips. "I did not realize you were so handsome a wench. Perhaps—" His eyes narrowed. "Perhaps, when we reach our destination, we may be able to discover some way to save you from what will otherwise be an unfortunate fate. What do you say, cutie?" he laughed, and reaching forward, chucked her under the chin. "Maybe you and I can get together?"

A slow, red flush crept over Nita's cheeks. Otherwise she gave no indication that she had heard him.

Reed raged in silent, helpless fury.

"We'll go now," Harker said. "You three go first. Samadu, change the tuning of the crystal to permit them to walk but do not permit them to cry out. No, wait, Reed. I want to talk to you a minute."

Samadu manipulated the crystal he was holding and the chiming of the tiny bells changed in tone. Deep in his body Reed felt a lessening of hellish pressures. Coiled tensions relaxed in his legs. A tingling, like that felt when a foot has gone to sleep, manifested itself. His breathing, which had been exceedingly difficult, became easier.

"Ladies first," Harker said politely. Nita, Adams, and Schultz walked out of the room. Samadu followed close behind them. He had thrust the hand holding the crystal into his coat pocket and the chiming coming from it was now muffled and indistinct. Apparently the radiations were no less effective, for the two men and the girl walked like stiff automatons who can barely drag their legs. To anyone watching them they were merely silent people walking down a hall. No threat was obvious, indeed Samadu's air, as he followed them, was one of casual indifference. Reed could not help wondering how often in the history of the Earth other men and other women had walked as these three walked, through crowds of people who did not suspect the hellish tragedy that was taking place.

He felt Harker's hand in his coat pocket.

"Your gun," Harker said. "You didn't think I'd forget that, did you? Of course I didn't want the others to see me take it from you because that might tell them you didn't really betray them. We wouldn't want them to know that, would we, especially the girl?"

"Y—y—you g—go to hell!" Reed rasped. It was all he could force out of his lips.

Harker grinned. He slapped the reporter on the shoulder. "Come, my good man," he said briskly. "We mustn't make the sons of destiny wait on us."

Reed walked stiffly out of the room. In his mind was a thunderous thought. Harker had taken his pistol. But Harker had completely forgotten to take the power bracelet away from him...

IN FRONT of the hotel they entered a taxicab. Nita, Adams, and Schultz sat in the back seat and Reed, Harker, and Samadu crowded into the jump seats. Harker gave his own address as their destination and the driver looked pleased. He was getting a long haul and with six people in his cab, he could expect a generous tip. Nita, Adams, and Schultz sat glumly, their faces showing only the muscular tension resulting from the effect of the radiations flowing from the crystal. Samadu sat silently. Harker beamed.

"A nice day, isn't it. Pleasantly cool and the air is very bracing this morning. Or at least I find it that way. Don't you?"

No one else found it that way.

They rode east from the Loop, passed over the viaduct above the Illinois Central tracks. Down below them Reed could see suburban trains shuttling into town, bringing the ten o'clock businessmen to their offices. Behind them the imposing skyline of Michigan Avenue was bright in the morning sun. They passed through Grant Park, turned south along the Lake Shore Drive.

A soft breeze was ruffling the surface of Lake Michigan. Far out two tiny sailboats, taking advantage of the breeze, were scudding along, their sails white against the soft green of the lake. Some mornings the lake was green, some mornings it was blue, and again it was gray, like a far-off hazy sky. It had a wide choice of colors, did this lake. This morning it was a soft green. Far out, the dim bulk of a ship was visible, an ore freighter hustling north for another load of Mesabi iron. The furnaces in South Chicago were hungry gluttons and no freighter charged with aiding in keeping their maws full of iron ore ever had time to rest.

Unconsciously Reed watched the familiar scenes unfold before his eyes. In his mind was the unconscious thought: would he ever see all this again? Was he looking for the last time at the skyline of Chicago, at the lake lapping gently against the huge stone blocks that guarded its shores? Nita, and those two strange men she had brought with her, were they also seeing all this for the last time? Schultz, in his thread-bare suit, Adams, who looked like a successful executive, and Nita Ayer, who looked like she belonged in the movies, were they looking their last at the world around them? Were they taking their last ride?

Were they on their way to the executioner? If they were taking their last ride, their faces showed no fear of it. What was it Harker had angrily said: "You sons of destiny, you are always cool and calm. Don't you know the meaning of fear?" At the time, Harker had thought Reed was a son of destiny, or had pretended to think so. It was hard to tell when Harker was pretending and when he was telling the truth but he had seemed to be telling the truth when he had indicated the sons of destiny were without fear. Certainly Schultz and Adams showed no trepidation. Reed wondered from what well of courage they drew their strength. What secret did they know that enabled them to ride to death without a tremor?

They drew up in front of Harker's residence. Samadu paid the driver, a twenty-dollar bill, and waved his hand to show that he wanted no change. The driver grinned happily.

INSIDE the house, Samadu directed Nita, Adams, and Schultz through a door at the rear of the entrance hall. Reed started to follow but Harker stopped him. "Come into my study," Harker said. "I want to talk to you."

Involuntarily the reporter looked up toward the ceiling, looking for the *hurthen*.

"You are searching for my little friend?" Harker said, interpreting his glance. "He is here all right but he is not so easy to see this morning. He shrinks from the full light of day, preferring to remain in shadows as much as possible. But let us not waste time discussing him. It was for another purpose that I brought you here. Sit down, man, and make yourself comfortable."

Reed stiffly sat down. Now that Samadu and the bells of the ringing crystals were gone, his body was again his to command. He looked at Harker, wondering what the man wanted now.

Harker sat down at his desk. There was a briskness about him like that of an executive who is about to embark on a big deal. He crossed his legs and looked thoughtfully at Reed. "You're a newspaper man, are you not?"

"Yes."

"A reporter, and I believe a good one."

"I'm a reporter. How good I am I leave to others to judge."

"Ah, yes... You work for the *Globe*, don't you?"

"Yes."

"Fine. How would you like to own the paper?"

Reed blinked. What nonsense was this? Own the *Globe!* The paper was worth millions! The owner was a millionaire. "What are you getting at?" the reporter said grumpily.

"I am, as you express it, getting at exactly what I said. How would you like to own the *Globe?*" Harker beamed fondly at Reed as though, in his opinion, he had asked a sensible question.

The reporter grinned. "Naturally I would like to own the *Globe,*" he said. "Will you buy it for me?"

"Yes," Harker said cheerfully.

Reed leaned back in his chair. Was Harker mad? Was he hooting crazy? Own the *Globe!*

"Of course you understand I will not really buy the paper for you. Direct purchase might be difficult. The owner is probably unwilling to sell. But if the owner should die, his widow would inherit the paper. I happen to know she is a flighty, hare-brained individual, totally unable to undertake the management of so valuable a piece of property. Under such circumstances, it would not be too difficult to manipulate the paper so that it would start losing money. Once the paper starts losing money, the widow would be eager to sell. With the backing of those whom I would send to you, it would not be difficult for you, an experienced, responsible newspaperman, to head a syndicate to purchase the paper, at our price. In this way control of the paper would pass completely into your hands."

REED stared in amazement at the man. It was a fiendishly ingenious scheme that Harker had proposed. Worst of all, it was a scheme that had an excellent chance of succeeding, once it was set in motion. John Hastings was the owner of the *Globe* and Mrs. Hastings was everything that Harker said she was. They had no children to inherit after them. If Mr. Hastings died, Mrs. Hastings could be relied on to make a mess of the newspaper that would fall into her hands. Reed shivered.

"Mr. Hastings," he casually observed, "to the best of my knowledge is enjoying excellent health. He is not likely to die merely to further your schemes."

"Isn't he?" Harker said. "Well, well. The truth is, Mr. Hastings has a bad heart, a condition that even his doctors do not suspect. While apparently enjoying excellent health, he is likely to drop dead any minute."

Reed sat in silence for a moment. "The truth is," he said slowly, "that Mr. Hastings is in first class physical condition and there is nothing wrong with his heart. The truth is, your scheme involves murdering him."

Harker shrugged. "If you want to put it that way, yes. But I assure you his death will be due to heart failure and I also assure you the best doctor in the country will not be able to say he did not die of heart failure." He spread his hands deprecatingly. "I have methods—"

"Ah," Reed said. His face was calm and impersonal. "Why do you pick me for this honor?" he asked. "Would it not be possible to find other tools better fitted to your needs?"

"I have picked you for two reasons," Harker answered. "One, you are already aware of my existence and my powers. Two, you have a hard, driving type of intelligence that appeals to me. As to your questions about finding someone else better fitted to my needs, it is not easy, even with the rewards I can offer, to find a capable man who is willing to serve me. I can use only the best. Fools will bungle my plans. You are not a fool, and I am frank to say, you would make a first-class assistant for me."

"Thank you," Reed said. "But there is one point that is not clear to me. If you give me the *Globe*, what do you get out of it? Where do you come in? What do you gain?"

Harker laughed. "A logical question, my boy. What do I get? I get control of the material published in your paper. The *Globe* is a powerful influence in this city and in this state. It has a large reader following and it can control and mould public opinion. I get control of its power."

Reed nodded He could understand this with no difficulty at all. The *Globe* was a crusading newspaper. It fought civic corruption, graft. Politicians contemplating putting a finger in the public till shuddered for fear that those lean, hot-eyed men employed by the *Globe* would discover what was going on and expose it in print. Gangsters left town hurriedly when the *Globe* got on their trail. Not a day dawned but that the editorial writers dipped their pens in gall and set out to joust with evil. There was no question but that a great liberal newspaper was a power for good in any community. There was no question in Reed's mind but that the *Globe* would cease to be a power for good, with Harker ordering the policies of the paper.

"Do you have any other questions?" Harker asked. "You must realize, my boy, that I want you to have a full and complete understanding of the situation. I want your full cooperation. Anything short of full cooperation is inadequate for my needs. Hence I welcome your questions."

"I have lots of questions," the reporter answered. "The biggest one is: Who is back of you? I do not for one minute believe that this is all your own idea. There must be someone back of you. Who is it?"

Harker's eyes glittered. "Are you sure you want that knowledge?" he asked.

"Quite sure," the reporter answered.

It was the one piece of knowledge that he desperately wanted. Who was back of Harker? From what source did he draw his tremendous powers?

HARKER'S fingers drummed on the desktop. His lips were pursed into a frown. "The One who is back of me," he said slowly, "is old on this earth. He was here before the earth was here. Names do not matter. In the long centuries He has had many names. Even I do not know His true name, or the full circumstances of His being. He does not choose to reveal this even to His most faithful followers, of which I count myself one. He sustains us. He gives us knowledge. He gives us power that we may work His will. Through Him are all things possible. But His name—" Harker paused and his voice dropped to a whisper as though he suspected the presence of a hidden listener who might overhear him. "His name I do not know. I can only call Him, as others call Him, the Power of Darkness."

His voice whispered into silence, and Reed, sitting stiffly in the chair, was aware of a feeling of coldness numbing every muscle in his body. The Power of Darkness! The Ancient One. Janicot. Eblis. He knew a few of the names bestowed upon this being. In his mind, ever since he realized the terrible strength that Harker possessed, was the fear that back of the man there could only be the Power of Darkness. A shuddering, soul-shaking fear! Now, from Harker's own lips, the fear was confirmed. Reed's heart turned to ice in his chest and cold winds blew over his body. He swallowed, fighting the fear that was in him.

"And I," he forced the tremor out of his voice, "as owner of the *Globe*, shall serve this One?" He questioned. "That is the pact you make with me?"

"Yes," Harker answered. "You shall serve me and through me, you shall serve Him."

Reed sat in silence. His face gave no indication of what was passing in his mind. Harker, watching him closely, saw this with approval. In seeking a new convert, Harker had chosen well. Harker needed men with steel nerves, men who could control themselves.

"Supposing," Reed said slowly, "supposing I pretend to accept, and then play you false? What means do you have for controlling me?"

Harker laughed. "You have seen my little friend?" he questioned. "Well, one of my little friends will go with you always. If ever you are tempted to disobey me, you will know that lurking near you is something that enforces my will. Under those conditions, I don't believe you can say I have no means of controlling you...can you?"

"No," Reed shuddered. His eyes went again to the corner of the room, where something gray and sinister might be lurking. Or might not be. "No."

"Any other questions?" Harker said briskly.

"Yes. Supposing—" the reporter's voice faltered. "Supposing I—I do not choose to accept your offer? What then?"

"Then," said Harker, "you are a dead man. Before you could hope to move from that chair, you are a dead man." He waved a hand. "I assure you, my little friend is near. I assure you he is ready and waiting eagerly."

As he spoke Reed felt a terrible coldness near him. The *hurthen*. It touched him, seemed to draw back. And if the *hurthen* failed, he didn't doubt Harker had other weapons at his command, other forces he could call into action.

"What do you say?" Harker asked.

"What can I say?" Reed answered. "That I accept your offer? Of course!"

"Good," said Harker briskly. "I anticipated that you would accept. In order that I may observe your loyalty, that you may give proof of your sincerity, I have saved a task for you to perform. Your first task for me. Think of it…the first of many tasks."

"W—what is it?" Reed choked.

"The execution of Adams, of Schultz, and of Nita Ayer," Harker answered. "Samadu is holding them in the basement. You shall have the privilege of executing them."

"The execution—"

Harker rose from his desk. He bowed politely. "You may precede me to the basement," he said. "Come now. Remember the wealth that is to be yours. Put a good face on this matter and precede me out of the room."

Reed rose slowly to his feet. Harker was taking him to the basement, to execute—his mind refused the thought completely. He could not, would not think, of executing Nita. But if he did not, Harker would certainly kill him.

## CHAPTER TEN
### *In the Basement*

A GLOOMY stairway led down to the basement and at the bottom there was a heavy oak door.

"Open up, Samadu," Harker called.

The door opened. Bowing, the Negro stood to one side. Reed entered the large, dimly lighted basement room. His first impression, confirmed by the sudden tension in his muscles, was the sound of the tiny bells ringing in the crystal. Samadu was holding his prisoners by means of the hellish radiations that paralyzed the muscles. Reed saw the prisoners. They were sitting quietly on a bench at one end of the room. Each of them was looking straight ahead but Nita glanced at him as he entered the basement, then looked quickly away. Reed could not look at her. He looked instead at the objects in the basement.

Set against the wall on one side was a complicated-looking device that somewhat resembled a compact but very powerful radio transmitter. Three heavy electrical cables ran from a switch on the wall into the device, apparently feeding current into it. Reed glanced at the set-up and the vague impression flitted across his mind that Harker was maintaining a secret radio transmitter. He looked for an antenna system and did not see one, unless the four posts rising a foot from the floor at the farther end of the room served the purpose of an aerial. The posts were of metal. They were set in insulated sockets in the concrete floor, forming an area about four feet square. Strands of metal cable connected their tops and two other strands of cable ran from them to the transmitter set against the wall.

The oddest object, the most nearly incomprehensible thing in the basement was—an ordinary springboard. Reed had seen hundreds of similar boards. Every swimming pool had two or three of them. Every rotogravure section ever printed in the country had a picture of at least one bathing beauty diving off such a board. This was a springboard all right. But there was no water under it. The only thing under it was the hard concrete of the basement floor. Its free end was about two feet above the concrete and was directly above the square area formed by the four metal posts. On the other side of the room eight or ten chairs, placed against the wall, were so arranged that persons sitting in them would form an audience for whatever took place here in this basement.

Reed stared in bewilderment around the place. He had expected to find instruments of torture here, the rack and the thumbscrew, torture devices more in keeping with Harker's sadistic viewpoint. Instead there was a diving board set above a concrete floor. Did Harker intend to force his victims to dive from the board and break their necks against the concrete? The idea was so crazy that it somehow brought relief of the frantic tension in Reed's mind. No, Harker was not going to execute his victims by having them jump off the board and break their necks by hitting the floor.

How was he going to execute them? How was he to be stopped? Reed's mind kept coming back to a single thought—the power bracelet in his coat pocket. There was strength in those moonstones bound in their circling metal.

The *hurthen* had fled from the bracelet and Harker had manifested a sincere respect for it. Nita had given it to him to protect him. Whether it sprang from magic or from cold, hard science, there was power in the bracelet.

The only difficulty was—*Reed did not know the secret of controlling that power!* He was like a savage who has found a high-power rifle in the jungle. Now the savage is faced with a lion. If he could use the rifle, bring it to his shoulder, release the safety, aim it, press the trigger gently, he could kill the lion and save his life. But if he can only think of the rifle as a rather strangely-shaped club and tries to use as he would use a club, he wastes the splendid power in the gun—and forfeits his own life. Reed could only think of the bracelet as a bracelet. He knew there was power in it but he did not know how to release the power, or what would happen if he did release it.

"Well, well," Harker said, beaming. "Here we are all together." He looked at the three sitting on the bench. "I can't begin to tell you how pleased I am to have you here. Many times I have dreamed of catching a single son of destiny but alas, until now good fortune has not come my way. Imagine my pleasure at capturing not one but *three* members of that organization at the same time! Three, mind you. Three at once."

HE SOUNDED quite happy about it. Then he looked across the room to the chairs against the wall and shook his head. "My colleagues would also relish witnessing this. I regret, however, that there is not time to summon them this morning. You understand," he bowed mockingly, "we sometimes hold little contests down here. My colleagues find these contests interesting and they will be annoyed when they learn one was held when they were not present."

No one spoke. The silence of the three on the bench seemed to irritate Harker but he kept his irritation under control. "Mr. Reed," he said suavely, "has volunteered to assist me in this contest."

"That's a dir—" The reporter caught himself. He had started to say, "That's a dirty lie!" but he managed to stifle the words before they left his lips.

"What did you say?" Harker demanded.

"Nothing," the reporter answered. The radiations from the crystal that Samadu held were getting to him. His muscles seemed to be slowly freezing. "I said," he whispered, "that darned crystal—can't you fix it so it doesn't affect me? I can barely move."

The glitter in Harker's eyes relaxed. For a moment he stared at Reed suspiciously. Then he reached into his pocket. The reporter caught his breath. Was Harker reaching for a gun?

Harker's hand appeared. It held an ordinary finger ring. "Forgive my forgetfulness," he said apologetically. "I had forgotten that you were not yet immune to the radiation. Put this ring on your finger. It will counteract the effect of the crystal."

Harker himself slipped the ring on Reed's hand. It looked like an ordinary signet ring of the kind worn by thousands of men but something had been built into it that no jeweler ever put into an ordinary ring. As soon as it was on his finger, his muscles began to thaw.

"Thank you," the reporter said huskily. He dared to breathe again. If Harker had not given him the means to counteract the effect of the radiations, he would not have been able to use the bracelet. Not that he knew how to use it anyhow, but as long as he could move, he could use it if he had a chance. And failing in the use of the bracelet, as a last resort he could throw himself at Harker's throat. He wondered how long he would live after that? Not long, he guessed, but that didn't matter, not if he could save Nita.

"I suggest," Harker said, "that we begin our contest." Beaming jovially, he moved to the radio transmitter set against the basement wall. The eyes of the three on the bench followed him. Now, for the first time, there was fear in them.

"Do you understand the little game we play down here?" Harker asked. "Ah, you don't understand it? That is too bad. You really must understand it so you can appreciate what is happening. First," he indicated the instrument beside which he was standing, "I close this switch, so."

He closed the switch. Immediately the soft hum of a transformer became audible in the room. Behind the dark panel of the transmitter, vacuum tubes began to glow with a dull, and then brilliantly crimson light.

"We must wait a few seconds for the tubes to warm," Harker explained. "Ah, I see they have already begun to heat."

HE GLANCED from the device to the four metal posts set in the floor. Reed followed the line of his gaze. Between the four posts, something—he could not tell exactly what was happening. At first he thought his eyes were blurring. From each post fingers of darkness were reaching out.

Reed gasped. Shocked recognition leaped into his mind. He had seen those fingers of darkness before. They had reached toward him when he had opened the door of

Harker's room and had tried to escape. They had lurked behind the windows, and Harker, when he recovered consciousness, had said they represented nothingness.

Had the veil of blackness that guarded the study above been generated here in this room? It seemed likely. At the time, the reporter thought he'd run headlong into black magic but it seemed now that the magic had a sound foundation in science. It was none the less real and hideous for all its scientific background.

From post to post the fingers of blackness reached, joined hands, spread out, until they formed a curtain of darkness four feet square. Black as a pool of ink, the ebony curtain hung a foot above the floor—and a foot below the end of the springboard.

Reed, remembering what Harker had told him about this blackness saw the horror that was lurking here. His flesh crawled.

Harker grinned. "Neat, isn't it?" he questioned. "I got the idea from a stunt the pirates used to pull in the old time. When the pirates had taken captives aboard their ship and had no further use for them, they had a clever way of getting rid of them. They lashed a strong plank to the deck, with the free end extending overboard—Ah, I see from your faces that you have caught the idea. Yes, this is a modern version of walking the plank. A person walks out to the end of the springboard and either steps off of his own will or is aided to step off—into the pool of blackness... What happens after that? I really have no idea." He chuckled deep in his throat. "I really have no idea what happens after that. *Something* happens. I am sure of that."

His grin reappeared. "How glum you look, you sons of destiny," Harker ejaculated. "How pleased my colleagues would be if they could only see your faces now."

He was a madman laughing at the horror his helpless victims felt. And yet it was not madness that motivated him. His power and his sadistic ruthlessness came not from madness but from One who dwelt in darkness.

"Are we all ready?" Harker called out. He left his place by the radio transmitter and came and stood in front of the three who sat silently on the bench. "Who shall be first?" he inquired, rubbing his hands together in a kind of sickening ecstasy. "Shall it be you?" he pointed at Adams. "Or you?" This time the finger was aimed at Schultz. "Or you?" He looked at Nita Ayer.

Silence was heavy in the room. Samadu, standing to one side and guarding the crystal, licked his lips in anticipation. He was cut from the same cloth as his master and what Harker enjoyed, Samadu would also enjoy.

"Would you like to go first?" Harker again asked the girl.

Her lips moved. A whisper was all she could utter. "I am ready," she said.

Harker looked slightly chagrined at her answer. He hid it with a smile. "Of course," he said, and his words dripped oil, "you really don't have to go at all. You're far too beautiful to step into the blackness. If you but say the word, you can stay here, with me."

Again her lips moved. "No…"

Harker was annoyed at this. "You fool. Don't you realize that black curtain is an entrance to another universe, that those who go into it enter into His realm? Don't you know that penetrating that curtain will blot you out completely?"

"I know," Nita said wanly. "I prefer that, to being false to the One to whom I owe allegiance. I prefer nothingness, to you."

SLOWLY, painfully, she rose to her feet. For a second Harker glared at her. Then he stalked over to the chairs placed against the wall. "If anyone should need assistance in walking the plank, Mr. Reed will provide it. He volunteered for that task, and I granted him the privilege. If anyone needs any urging, Mr. Reed will provide that too. On with the show."

Crossing his legs, Harker leaned his chair back against the wall.

Slowly, as though every move was an effort, Nita stepped on the springboard. She stumbled and almost fell.

"Here, Nita, let me help you," Reed said. He sprang to her side tried to take her arm.

She shook his hand aside. "No thank you, Mr. Reed. I do not need any help from you, either."

"But you do—"

"No! Keep your hands off of me. I've come this far by myself and I can go the rest of the way."

She looked at the reporter and through him and did not see him.

"Nita—" he whispered. There was desperation in his voice. As soon as he realized the purpose of the springboard and the part he was to play in the performance, he had conceived of a plan that might, possibly, save the situation. His plan was to help Nita as she walked along the board, to take her arm and offer his assistance. While he was doing this he would slip her the power bracelet. She would know how to use it. Harker, across the room, would not see what was happening until the bracelet was in her possession.

But in order to keep Harker from seeing him slip the bracelet to her, he had to pretend to help her along the plank.

She wouldn't accept his help, though. She wouldn't let him take her arm. She wouldn't let him touch her!

"Don't speak to me," she whispered. "I—I thought—you—" There were tears in her eyes.

Harker seemed to enjoy the scene. "Very good!" he called out, clapping loudly.

"Let me help you, Nita," the reporter begged.

"You want to help me—to that?" She nodded toward the inky pool a foot above the floor.

Reed could not speak.

"Of course he wants to assist you to the opening..." Harker called out. "it is the last thing he will ever be able to do for you. Come, my dear. Take his arm and stroll down to the end of the plank. When you reach the end, he can have the pleasure of shoving you off." The idea was apparently very pleasing to him for he roared with laughter.

"Would you shove me off?" Nita asked.

"No," Reed whispered desperately. "Listen, Nita—"

"What are you saying?" Harker called out abruptly. "Speak louder. I don't want to miss a word of this."

The girl looked irresolutely from Harker to Reed. "I'm just making a show for you to enjoy," she whispered. "Well, I won't make a show any longer..." She started walking along the springboard.

Reed grabbed her arm. "Not so fast," he said. "Mr. Harker and I are enjoying this. We want it to last as long as possible."

He thrust the bracelet into her hand.

She felt the warmth of the moonstones against her skin. A little start passed through her body. She stopped trying to pull free. Her eyes darted to Reed's face, held there with an intensity he had never seen before. Then, as though to reassure herself that what she thought had happened was really true, she glanced down at the object he had pressed into her hand—and saw the moonstones glowing softly with that subtle inward light they seemed to possess.

For a split second, while Reed watched, she stopped breathing.

IT WAS one of the few times in his life when Reed was praying. Was there the power in the bracelet that he thought was there? Was there enough power, in some incredible way, to overcome Harker? Was the power usable? Or had he waited too long to give her the bracelet? Like the savage with the gun, he could only thrust what he knew was a weapon into the hands of one who knew how to use it, and hope somehow that the gun would stop the lion.

Nita did not move. She stared at the bracelet.

With a crash, Harker's chair came down on the floor. "What's going on there?" he demanded. "What are you trying to do, Reed? I saw you slip something to her? What was it?"

Nita glanced at the reporter. There had been tears in her eyes. Now the tears, miraculously, had turned to stars. "Oh, Don—" she whispered.

"If you know how to use that thing, for Pete's sake use it..." the reporter gasped. "This is our last chance."

"Reed!" Harker shouted. "Damn you—if you've double-crossed me... Samadu!"

He continued shouting for his giant servant.

Nita's fingers slid along the bracelet. She touched one of the moonstones, turned it, ever so slightly, in its setting. Bright lights gleamed in the gems, flashed up like miniature searchlights probing a far-away sky.

Instantly the room was full of sound. Always in the background had been the muted chiming of the bells ringing in the crystal. Now there was a new sound. Now another set of tiny bells were ringing. Bells in the moonstones, as clear and clean and sweet as bells from fairyland. The bells ringing in the moonstones seemed to be fighting the bells ringing in the crystal. There was a clash of tones, a furious ringing, like the sounds of battle far away. There was a sense of struggle, of pushing and shoving, of two antagonists meeting sword and buckler. There was no other sound in the room. It was as though everyone present had stopped dead still and was waiting the result of some furious far-off battle on which their fate depended. Harker seemed to have become paralyzed. He was staring at the bracelet Nita was holding and he didn't seem to believe the evidence of his eyes. He knew it was not possible for her to have a bracelet. Yet she had one.

Too late Harker remembered he had failed to take the bracelet from Reed, "Damn you…" he cursed. "Samadu!"

The giant servant had turned an ashen gray. He had pulled the crystal from his pocket and he was frantically working with it, trying to change or adjust it.

Bell sounds swirled angrily in the room. The bells ringing in the moonstones seemed to grow louder. As they grew louder, the bells from the crystal grew weaker. There was a final swirl of furious chiming. Then there was a clink as if some object—caught in enormous pressures—was breaking.

SAMADU stared at the crystal in his hand. At the final *clink* the crystal had crumbled into fragments. No sound came from it. The only sound in the room was the ringing of the bells in the moonstones. They were ringing triumphantly now!

The silence held for an infinitesimal part of a second. Then there was a scrape, as of some heavy object being kicked aside. Out of the corner of his eye Reed glimpsed Adams and Schultz rising from the bench, kicking it away from them, leaping to their feet. The breaking of the crystal had freed them from their paralysis. At the same instant he saw Harker reaching into his pocket.

Reed hurled himself across the basement—toward Harker. His left fist, with all the momentum of his charge behind it, went into Harker's stomach.

Harper gasped in pain. He had succeeded in getting his hand out of his pocket and as Reed struck him, something flew from his hand and clattered on the floor. Harker dived after it. The reporter drove his shoulder into him and rammed with all his strength. Caught off balance, Harker crashed into the basement wall. Reed started to hit him again, but as he drew back, he was aware of something rushing between them. Schultz! Like a great shaggy dog, he grabbed at Harker's throat.

Vaguely Reed was aware that Adams had chosen Samadu. Sounds of furious conflict came from the pair, thuds of fists meeting flesh, grunts of pain.

Harker clawed at Schultz, seemed to slip, and both of them fell heavily to the floor. They fought in silence, with a ferocity that was appalling. Neither of them was asking quarter, nor would it have been given. The stakes in this fight were mortal. Schultz had Harker by the throat and he hung on. Harker was underneath. He bent his body like a bow, hurled Schultz upward, brought up a knee that struck the other in the groin. Schultz lost his grip and his face turned gray with pain. The blow had been foul, but that didn't matter in this fight. The struggle here was for survival and for something bigger than survival. No holds were barred. Harker, breathing heavily, struggled to his feet.

Reed was waiting. He stepped forward, his left coming up. Under the impetus of the blow, Harker staggered against the wall. The reporter closed in. Mercilessly he rammed home the blows. *Smack! Smack! Smack!* One after the other, stomach, chin, jaw. Harker struck back at him but the blows were feeble. Strength was going out of the man but hate was not. Reed could sense the hatred with which Harker was trying to fight. Bitter, blinding, burning hate—there was nothing else left in him.

Reed drove his fist home at the corner of the jaw. Harker collapsed. Breathing heavily, the reporter stepped backward. Adams and Samadu were still struggling. When Harker collapsed, Samadu seemed to lose all his courage. He turned, clawed at the basement door, jerked it open, and ran heavily up the stairs. Adams followed him. Their feet pounded on the floor overhead. There was a heavy thud as the front door was slammed. Samadu had run and Harker was unconscious.

Reed looked around. Nita had not moved from her position on the springboard. "Times looked kind of tough for the home team, didn't they?" he said. "I thought we were a bunch of goners."

"We would have been, if you hadn't had this," she held up the bracelet. Suddenly she screamed. Reed whirled.

Harker was on his feet again. The man had been playing possum. He hadn't been knocked out. Feet planted wide apart, Harker was standing with his back against the wall. Oddly though—even with the basement door open—he made no effort to escape.

From his lips a torrent of words were pouring, a chant, an invocation to some dark deity. The words were not English. High and shrill, they echoed through the room. Abruptly they ended.

"So you thought you had beaten me?" Harker said viciously. "So you thought you had won…"

Answering his chant, answering his invocation, something came from the pool of blackness still hanging above the floor at the end of the springboard. Reed caught a glimpse of it as it emerged. Then he could see it no longer—but he knew what it was. A *hurthen!* Before he could move he saw the blackness swirl again and another of the fierce little monstrosities sprang upward into the air.

*Hurthen!* The *hurthen* came from beyond the blackness. That was their home. They belonged there. Harker had summoned them to his aid.

"Now what are you going to do?" Harker shouted.

Nita was frantically manipulating the bracelet that she held.

"The power of the bracelet will stop one *hurthen*," Harker yelled. "But it won't stop a dozen of them. Ah… More of my little friends are coming."

OUT of the pool of blackness two of the *hurthen* leaped at the same time, leaped upward, were visible for an instant, and then vanished. As they came, the room seemed suddenly to be growing appreciably colder.

Reed hurled himself at the man. In his mind, somehow, was the thought that if he could hit Harker he could stop the *hurthen* from appearing. He was aware that Schultz had staggered to his feet and was trying to help him.

"Pick him up!" Schultz was yelling. "Lift him off the floor."

Harker kicked at them. Reed dodged and moved in. The man's fists flailed off the reporter's head. Somehow Reed managed to lift him off the floor.

"Hurry!" Nita called frantically. "There are too many *hurthen*. I can't keep them all away."

"I've got him!" the reporter yelled. "But what in the hell am I going to do with him?"

He was aware that Schultz was tugging and pushing at him. "Over there!" Schultz shouted. "Over there."

Reed understood. With Schultz helping him, he held Harker above the floor and staggered across the room. Harker realized what was about to happen. He screamed and kicked, slugged, and tried to bite. Reed doggedly held on. Suddenly both he and Schultz let go. Harker fell.

He fell straight into the pool of blackness that hung in the air below the end of the springboard. He was screaming as he fell. His body writhed as he tried to find a grip on the air with which to hold himself away from what was below him. He hit the blackness. It boiled like smoke caught in a whirlwind. He went out of sight into the blackness. The evil closed over him. His screams went into sudden silence.

There was a blur in the air above the veil. *Hurthen*, diving downward into it, were either following their master into the darkness to serve him in the universe that he had said was beyond the nothingness of the veil, or—what was more probably—like carrion-scenting vultures were diving in to feast off him. Schultz watched them go. When the last one had gone, he staggered over to the device that looked like a radio transmitter and cut the switches.

The pool of blackness collapsed.

"Very good," said a voice from the doorway. It was Adams who had spoken. The man was out of breath. "Samadu got away," he said. "I chased him but I couldn't—catch him. Very fine, what you did to Harker. Oh, very fine indeed. He'll feast in his own hell tonight, which is exactly where he belongs."

Reed suddenly sat down. He stared from one to the other. "Would you mind," he panted. "Would you mind telling me what this is all about?"

## CHAPTER ELEVEN
### *Don Reed Persists*

REED opened the door of the old house. Nita smiled at him and passed through. He followed her. She took his arm and they went down the steps together. Adams and Schultz, looking something like grim, gray watchdogs, came behind them.

They left behind them in the basement a piece of electrical equipment that looked like a radio transmitter but wasn't. It had been thoroughly and efficiently smashed. Schultz had seen to that. The house had been thoroughly searched. Adams and Schultz had taken care of that. Reed did not know what they had found, if anything. He had spent the time listening to the story Nita was telling him. The story was not finished. It would probably never be finished.

"The sons of destiny have had many names," Nita had said. "We prefer to be thought of as watchmen, for that

192

word more nearly expresses the nature of our task. We are at least as old as the human race on this planet and possibly older. That point is not completely clear."

"You mean you—" the reporter protested. "You mean *you* are thousands, hundreds of thousands of years old?" He did not want to accept this thought. It was somehow, repellent to him.

The girl laughed. "Of course not, silly. I'm just as old as I look, and if you want to consult the records, I was born in a little town in Indiana. My father and mother are there still."

Reed was relieved to hear this. He'd been afraid that Nita was—well, he had seen her vanish and he knew that she belonged to an organization that she had said was thousands of years old. Always he had been afraid she was not quite human. A weight lifted from his mind when he learned she was.

"The *organization* is as old as the human race, not its members. The persons who belong to it are quite ordinary people. We are born, we die. The group recruits new members to take up the task of those who can no longer do their job."

"What is this job?" Reed asked.

"To watch by night," the girl answered. "To keep guard against the things that go in the night, to make certain that when morning comes the things we put away at dusk will be safe."

Reed knew that she spoke figuratively, but it seemed to him that the figure of speech was uncommonly apt. To watch by night! To his mind came the picture of shepherds guarding their flocks during the hours of darkness. Wolves, and other bad things, came in the night. The shepherds had to ward off the wolves. The sons of destiny were watchmen who guarded the night. He had suspected as much. It made him feel good to know that somewhere there were watchmen.

"Harker and the One whom he served," Nita shuddered when she mentioned the One whom Harker served. "Seek to corrupt and destroy. Our name for the One whom Harker served is the Antagonist, the Enemy. In the days that have gone He has had many servants. Harker was but one servant. We, in turn, have our Master, whom we serve."

SHE paused there and seemed to be groping for words. When she continued, she spoke slowly. "To understand our part, the part of our Master, the part Harker played, and the part of the Antagonist, is to understand the full purpose of human life on earth, its origin, its meaning, and its destiny. I do not fully understand—the scale is too vast. The earth is a stage, in a setting that involves millions of years of time, a space as high as the sky is high. On this stage drama is in progress. We humans, all of us, are actors in this drama. Somewhere behind the scenes, completely off the stage we occupy, our Master and the Antagonist are striving with each other to determine the course the drama shall take, and its final outcome."

In Reed's mind were words. "All the world's a stage and the men and women merely players. Each has his exits and his entrances—"

"Another way to think of it is to visualize a planted field," Nita continued. "A field of corn. The ground is plowed and harrowed, the seed-bed prepared. The seed is planted. Showers come. The grain sprouts, begins to grow. All over the field, tender green shoots begin to appear. The corn is growing. But it must be cultivated, it must be protected. The crows would pull up the tender shoots, the corn borer would attack the ripening ears. Cattle might break into the field—"

She paused. "You must conceive of the stalks of corn being intelligent enough to aid the planter in protecting them. They must give warning when danger comes. Some of them must fight against that danger. Do you follow me?"

"With difficulty," Reed answered.

"The horrors that walk in Europe and in Asia, these are also difficult to understand, are they not?" she answered.

The reporter stared at her. "You mean—"

She nodded. "The One whom Harker served has other servants. They have loosed this destruction. They have loosed it all over the globe." Irrelevantly she changed the subject. "What did Harker offer you when he wanted you to join him?"

"A newspaper…"

"Yes, that sounds like him! The one thing he would most like to control. With it he could sway public opinion, divide us, possibly make us fight each other. The Antagonist would be that much the gainer. He is very clever."

Reed stared grimly at her. There were other questions he wanted to ask, hundreds of them. She answered them without hesitation. The bracelets were made by an obscure technician—obscure so far as publicity was concerned—who was also a watchman of the night. They enabled their wearers to instantaneously transport themselves from one place to another. She had used the power in her bracelet to escape from the assassin who had tried to kill her on the street. Reed had witnessed this murder. She had also used it to escape from jail. The secret of the bracelets was old.

In various forms they had been made for thousands of years, the technical details of their construction being passed on from generation to generation. Merthu had been a messenger, sent from the Master. Yes, messengers were sometimes sent, when the struggle was difficult and the world was in turmoil, to aid in the conflict. Was it possible that Joan of Arc and others like her had been such messengers? Nita did not know. She thought it probable. Unfortunately Harker had somehow learned of the coming of the messenger and had destroyed him. No, it was not possible to tell when or where such a messenger would come, or how he would arrive. They had to be on the watch for him. They had to be on the watch for many things.

"But Harker," Reed protested. "When I first met him, he said he came from the hidden world."

"That was the one thing you and no one else would be willing to believe," Nita answered. "He represented the hidden world. He could tell the truth in perfect safety because no one would believe him."

"I guess," the reporter mused, "I guess that is why the sons of destiny, the watchmen of the night, do not advertise their presence. No one would believe them."

"That is one reason," Nita admitted, a little sadly. "There is another reason but I do not have the time to explain it now. Any other questions?"

"Hundreds of them," Reed answered. "I'll ask them later."


THEY strolled down the walk outside the house. The sounds, the sights, the smells of the city struck the reporter like a blow. Streetcars rattling, cars honking, newsboys shouting the noon edition of the papers. Oblivious of their presence, the world went on.

Reed turned to the girl. "How," he demanded, "does one get to belong to your organization?"

"By refusing to take 'No' for an answer," she said. "It is not easy to join. Harder even than joining is discovering that it exists. You have to look at the world around you and see the things going on in it. No matter where you look, you will see signs of the struggle between our Master and the Antagonist, the battle which is being fought here with the whole world as a stage. You will begin to wonder why this fight goes on, why living is such a struggle. Eventually you will begin to get hints that some supernatural battle is in progress here on earth. You will want to take sides in this battle. If you are very discerning, you will reason that some kind of an organization must be hidden out of sight somewhere. You will begin searching for this organization. If you discover it, you will find you have already joined it."

"Hey? What's this. If you discover it, you have already joined it?"

"You joined long ago," Nita Ayer said. "When you began digging up crooks and exposing politicians and doing all the thousand and one things that a good reporter does, you joined the organization."

Deep lines of thought furrowed Reed's forehead. He saw, at last, one of the hidden motives that had governed his whole life. Somehow the knowledge made him feel good all over.

"But," he persisted. "The watchers—like Schultz and Adams—and you! How does one become one of these?"

"By persisting," Nita Ayer answered. "You must realize that such an organization *must* exist. Then you have to

197

begin hunting for it. If you search hard enough, you will find someone who belongs to it. You will tell him you want to join."

"Ah!"

"He will say you are a fool, that no such group exists. He will insist he is right and you are wrong. But you will persist. You will not give up. You will keep on trying. All the time you are doing this, you are being tested. If you are not found wanting, you will become a Watcher."

Reed was silent. "Have I persisted long enough?" he asked.

"Yes," Nita Ayer said.

"There are a lot of things I don't know," he continued.

"I will teach you," she answered.

They came down the sidewalk of the old house, and at the street they turned right. Adams and Schultz looked thoughtfully after them for a moment. Then they grinned and turned and walked in the other direction.

To the casual passerby they were a young couple strolling along the street at noon, such a young couple as might logically be looking for an apartment, a place to live, a spot to call home. Adams and Schultz, going in the other direction, were a couple of middle-aged men returning to work after lunch, the duties of the afternoon before them.

NOW and again Don Reed and Nita Ayer—the name on the mailbox of the neat apartment they occupy is Mr. and Mrs. Donald Reed—in answer to a summons that comes to them by no ordinary means, dress quietly and go forth into the night. They go together, these two, always together, as though they are afraid of being separated from each other. They go forth to danger, but when the summons comes, they do not hesitate. There is work to be done.    They remember the chairs placed along the basement wall in the house that Harker occupied.   Those chairs mean that Harker had helpers, assistants, colleagues, who must be found.

The search for Harker's helpers goes quietly on.   And will go on.   As always, since the time the earth first started rolling, there are Watchers in the night.

## THE END

*If you've enjoyed this book, you will not want to miss these terrific titles…*

## ARMCHAIR SCI-FI & HORROR DOUBLE NOVELS, $12.95 each

**D-71**    **THE DEEP END** by Gregory Luce
         **TO WATCH BY NIGHT** by Robert Moore Williams

**D-72**    **SWORDSMAN OF LOST TERRA** by Poul Anderson
         **PLANET OF GHOSTS** by David V. Reed

**D-73**    **MOON OF BATTLE** by J. J. Allerton
         **THE MUTANT WEAPON** by Murray Leinster

**D-74**    **OLD SPACEMEN NEVER DIE!** John Jakes
         **RETURN TO EARTH** by Bryan Berry

**D-75**    **OPERATION INTERSTELLAR** by George O. Smith
         **THE THING FROM UNDERNEATH** by Milton Lesser

**D-76**    **THE BURNING WORLD** by Algis Budrys
         **FOREVER IS TOO LONG** by Chester S. Geier

**D-77**    **THE COSMIC JUNKMAN** by Rog Phillips
         **THE ULTIMATE WEAPON** by John W. Campbell

**D-78**    **THE TIES OF EARTH** by James H. Schmitz
         **CUE FOR QUIET** by Thomas L. Sherred

**D-79**    **SECRET OF THE MARTIANS** by Paul W. Fairman
         **THE VARIABLE MAN** by Philip K. Dick

**D-80**    **THE GREEN GIRL** by Jack Williamson
         **THE ROBOT PERIL** by Don Wilcox

## ARMCHAIR SCIENCE FICTION CLASSICS, $12.95 each

**C-25**    **THE STAR KINGS**
         by Edmond Hamilton

**C-26**    **NOT IN SOLITUDE**
         by Kenneth Gantz

**C-32**    **PROMETHEUS II**
         by S. J. Byrne

## ARMCHAIR SCIENCE FICTION & HORROR GEMS SERIES, $12.95 each

**G-7**    **SCIENCE FICTION GEMS, Vol. Seven**
         Jack Sharkey and others

**G-8**    **HORROR GEMS, Vol. Eight**
         Seabury Quinn and others